MUFFINS AFTER MAGIC

LATTES AND LEVITATION - BOOK 2

CHRISTINE POPE

MUFFINS AFTER MAGIC

CHAPTER 1

Mazes and Muffins

"Ready for your big date, Skye?" my friend Deanne teased me as she slid a tray of pumpkin chocolate chunk muffins into the bakery case.

I did my best not to shoot her a jaundiced look. Judging by the way her mouth pursed in amusement after she asked the question, I didn't think I'd been too successful at hiding my feelings.

"It's not a *date*," I said, my tone a little too severe. "Max just didn't want to go to the harvest festival by himself."

"Hmm," Deanne replied, which could have meant anything...but I guessed was her way of saying she didn't believe me for a second, even if she wasn't going to come right out and tell me I was full of horse manure.

As much as she—and I—might have hoped the

outing Max Sullivan and I had planned for tomorrow night was truly a date, I knew better. Ever since I'd helped him clear his name in the death of Perry Lockhart, the director of the film Max had been working on in our hometown of Las Vegas, New Mexico, when Perry was murdered, he'd been super-friendly...but that's *all* he'd been. We'd gone out to eat several times in the weeks that had followed the D.A.'s dropping of the first-degree murder charges, and Max had invited me over to Sunset Ridge, the ranch he'd bought once he decided he was missing the whole small-town experience and wanted to spend more time away from the hustle and bustle of Hollywood, but there hadn't been anything remotely romantic about the time we'd spent together.

No, we'd talked about the projects he had coming up on his calendar, and about his plans to build some stables on the property and buy horses, but he'd never once tried to lean in for a goodnight kiss, and had never so much as even reached out to touch my hand. It was clear enough to me that he saw me as a friend and nothing more, no matter what the town gossips—or my best friend Deanne —might have to say on the subject.

And I did my best to tell myself that was okay. Maybe one day he'd have an epiphany and realize the perfect woman for him had been right under his nose all long...or maybe he wouldn't. In the meantime, I'd do my best to simply enjoy his company, something I'd been missing for the past ten years, ever since he'd left college his sophomore year to pursue his Hollywood dreams.

A month had passed since that fateful day in September when Evan Bryant, the husband of Max's high school girlfriend Raylene Brown, had killed Perry Lockhart in an attempt to frame Max for the director's murder. The plan had backfired on him, mainly because a tea leaf reading I'd performed had pointed me in the direction of the actual killer, and Evan had ended up getting charged with first-degree murder—and aggravated assault as well, since he'd pulled a gun on me once he figured out I'd been asking questions he definitely didn't want answered.

To everyone's relief...well, except Raylene's, I suppose...the murder had been pretty much an open-and-shut case, and the trial had lasted only two days. A jury found Evan guilty on all charges, and he was now safely locked up in the Central New Mexico Correctional Facility. Since he'd been given a life sentence without the possibility of parole, he was no longer a problem for Max or anyone else.

And even though her husband had tried to kill him, Max had been worried about Raylene, now left with three young children to raise on her own. True, her father-in-law had given her his son's former sales manager position at the Ford dealership he owned, so the little family wasn't left to fend for themselves. However, Max obviously thought that wasn't nearly enough to ensure a comfortable existence for the young Bryants, because he also created a trust fund for the kids, one that would ensure they could all go to college if they wanted, and made sure Raylene had enough access to the funds that she could cover the cost of childcare now that she was working full-time.

It seemed she wasn't entirely broken up about Evan's misdeeds, because almost as soon as he was sentenced, she commenced divorce proceedings against him. Maybe that was the sensible thing to do, but since she also joined a local gym and seemed to be working at getting herself back to her high school glory days as quickly as possible, I had to believe she only planned to work at the dealership long enough to find a new husband so she could go back to being a stay-at-home mom.

Which...more power to her, I supposed. The few times our paths had crossed since Evan's arrest, she'd given me the evil eye and quickly found somewhere else she needed to be, telling me she obviously blamed me for her soon-to-be-ex's current situation. Never mind that he'd been the one to cook up the scheme, and the one who'd pulled the trigger. No, it was crazy Skye O'Malley, the weirdo who read tea leaves, who'd brought about his downfall.

Whatever. Raylene and I hadn't been besties even before I helped bring her husband to justice, so it wasn't as though I was going to cry bitter tears over being cut out of her life. All the same, it was hard not to notice how she hadn't extended that same social exile to Max, who was the one who'd tackled Evan and zip-tied him so he wouldn't be able to get away before the police showed up. I had no doubt that if Max had so much as crooked his little finger, she would have come running, convinced he was ready to return to the good old days when they'd been boyfriend and girlfriend.

To my infinite relief, he showed no sign of doing any such thing. In fact, once he got the trust set up for Raylene's family, he seemed all too glad to do whatever he could to stay out of her orbit. Since the ranch he'd bought was located outside Las Vegas's city limits, and he only seemed to come into town to drop into the coffee shop or maybe have dinner with his parents, whose home was located right next door to mine, that wasn't too difficult a task for him to accomplish.

Because although he'd seriously cut down his security detail, Max had kept Lou D'Amato, one of the bodyguards from Albuquerque he'd hired a month earlier, on the payroll, along with a guy named Al Torres. They seemed to spell each other keeping an eye on their boss and on the expensive property he'd bought, and also seemed to do most of his fetching and carrying.

At least, I had yet to bump into my friend at Walmart, or at one of the local gas stations.

That sort of behavior would have made most of the locals raise an eyebrow, but even though Max was a hometown boy, he'd spent the past decade away in Los Angeles building his film and television career, and now that he was one of the world's top box office draws, everyone in town probably assumed it was natural for a celebrity like him to have someone else run his errands.

The door to Levitation Latte—my somewhat whimsically named coffee shop—opened then, and in strode the mayor, Tom Gallegos. He was about fifteen years Deanne's and my senior, putting him in his early forties, and he was the kind of overly energetic type who did a good job as steward of the town but who was always a little exhausting to be around. His dark hair still didn't show any signs of gray, but although he was tall, he'd begun to sport a bit of a paunch these last couple of years.

"Skye," he said, striding up to me where I stood behind the counter, "all set for tomorrow?"

"Absolutely," I replied.

The mayor wasn't referring to my not-date with Max, of course. No, the next day was Las Vegas's harvest festival, even more of an event this year because it would be the hundredth anniversary of the town's first harvest celebration, held way back in the early 1920s. My Grandma Maureen, who'd owned the coffee shop before she passed away and left it to me, had been a fixture at the event, serving coffee and hot spiced cider and cookies, and I'd taken over those duties these past couple of years.

Luckily, Deanne and her husband Mike would also be working the Levitation Latte booth the following evening, which would leave me free to spend some time with Max. Of course, he'd attended the harvest festival back when he lived here, but the event had continued to expand and get more elaborate during the decade he'd been gone, and so he wanted to experience the new and improved version for himself.

"You wouldn't let me go through that corn maze by myself, would you?" he'd asked when coaxing me to leave the coffee shop's booth for an hour or so, and, being the pushover I was, of course I'd agreed to spend some time with him...even as I'd slyly asked whether he would truly have been alone, considering he seemed to have either Lou or Al lurking somewhere in the background most of the time.

"You'll never even notice they're there," Max had assured me, and I'd just had to laugh.

Anyway, I felt pretty confident telling Mayor

Gallegos I had everything in hand. "And," I added, "we're going to be serving pumpkin spice lattes along with the regular coffee and cider, so I think it'll be a treat for everyone."

He gave an approving nod. "That sounds good," he said. "And you're sure you can be there for setup at three?"

This time, Deanne stepped in...probably because she could tell I was a little annoyed at the implication that I didn't have everything taken care of. Tom Gallegos probably hadn't meant any offense, but he had a well-deserved reputation as a micro-manager.

"Or even a little before three," she said. "Remember, we're not open on Saturdays, so we have all day to get everything prepped before we take it over to the park."

He didn't exactly relax...but at least he apparently decided to stop fussing over us, which I had to take as a good sign.

"Good to hear," he said briskly. "Oh, and I just found out that reporters from Santa Fe and even Albuquerque are coming to cover the event, since it's our centennial. We have to make sure everything goes off without a hitch."

"And it will," Deanne replied, her tone soothing.

I managed a smile and said, "It's going to be great."

Those combined reassurances appeared to be enough to placate him. Or at least, his iWatch pinged, and he looked down at its screen before saying, "It sounds like you've got everything covered. I'm off to check on the setup for the corn maze. See you tomorrow."

He hurried out, gaze still fixed on his left wrist.

After the door closed behind him, I released a breath.

"I don't envy Cory Sills her job," I remarked, referring to the woman who was Tom's office assistant and right-hand woman. She'd been two years ahead of us in high school, so we weren't super close or anything, but I knew her well enough to know the mayor generally ran her ragged.

Deanne grinned. "Me, neither. But since she's also kind of Type A, I think she thrives on it."

One would think that a small town like Las Vegas—currently boasting a population of a little over thirteen thousand people—wouldn't have much need of Type A personalities, since life tended to run at a slower pace in these parts. But I supposed you got people like that no matter where you lived, although I certainly couldn't count myself as one of them. No, I was just fine with taking some time to smell the flowers...or at least, to allow myself to sit at my kitchen table and enjoy a cup of tea.

"Maybe she does," I said, and paused. "You're really sure Mike is okay with watching the Levitation Latte booth tomorrow night?"

Deanne's brow creased a bit, although I could tell her expression of annoyance was mostly feigned. "For the hundredth time, yes. After all, you can only walk a corn maze so many times, and he's not much into the kiddie games or the craft booths."

No, probably not. Mike was the nicest guy in the world, but as accommodating as he tended to be, he definitely wasn't the type to care much about inspecting a bunch of quilts or buying someone's homemade goat's milk soap. At least babysitting our booth would give him something to do, since he was the kind of person who could chat up people he'd known his entire life and still discover something new and interesting about each and every one of them.

"Okay," I said. "And there's no problem with you coming in at one o'clock to help with the baking?"

We'd already made plans to come to the shop to prep all the muffins and cookies we'd be selling at the booth, since the kitchen at Levitation Latte was so much better suited to making large batches of baked goods. From here, we could box everything up and take it directly to Plaza Park, located only steps from the coffee shop.

I'd actually wondered if the coordinators were going to be able to fit everything that had been planned into the park, since it wasn't Las Vegas's biggest public space by any stretch of the imagination. However, the tradition was for the harvest festival to be held there, and somehow they'd managed to shoehorn everything—corn maze included—into the available acreage.

"No problem at all," Deanne replied at once. "I already told Mike he's on laundry duty that day, but he assured me he could handle it."

Well, one would hope so. He was a grown man of thirty, after all.

That thought got me wondering if Max also did his own laundry, or whether he made Al or Lou manage that particular duty. The mental image of either of those big, burly guys carefully measuring out fabric softener and folding underwear made me want to laugh, and I guessed that Max probably roughed it and took care of all the domestic duties while he was living here in Las Vegas. In all the times I'd been over at the ranch, I'd certainly never seen any evidence that he'd hired any help beyond the two bodyguards, although I guessed he must have someone come in to clean from time to time, and probably had retained the services of some gardeners as well. The property was too pristine for me to imagine otherwise, since Max had never showed any affection for yard duty back when he was living at home.

"All right, then," I said. "It sounds like we've got everything ready to go."

"Absolutely," Deanne said stoutly. "You know it's going to all go off without a hitch."

Well, the harvest festival would run smoothly enough.

Whether I could say the same about my not-exactly-a-date with Max remained to be seen.

CHAPTER 2

Cookie Monster

Because Deanne and I planned to go straight over to the festival after our frenzy of baking at Levitation Latte, I brought along a tote bag with a change of clothes and some makeup, since I wouldn't have time to go home and change out of my floury T-shirt and jeans. We made chocolate chip cookies and snickerdoodles, pumpkin walnut muffins and blueberry ones as well, even though I had to admit there wasn't anything particularly harvest-y about those. But they were perennial favorites, and I knew that leaving them off the menu probably wasn't a very good idea.

Deanne had also brought some fresh clothes to change into, although she didn't seem too concerned about her hair and makeup. To her credit, she didn't comment as I proceeded to brush on mascara and lip gloss once we were done baking...although her mouth twitched a bit.

We'd known each other almost all our lives, ever since we'd met in third grade after her family moved to Las Vegas from Tucumcari. Why exactly she'd decided to befriend me, the skinny, dark ugly duckling in our class, rather than one of the popular girls—Deanne was almost model-pretty, with big blue eyes and light blonde hair, and probably could have fit into that group very easily—I'd never been able to quite figure out.

Actually, scratch that. Although she hadn't started a family yet, she had a maternal streak a mile wide, and even though she'd been the new girl, she'd somehow guessed right away that I was someone who needed protection from the class bullies. My grandmother had raised me, since my mom bailed out when I was only an infant and my father had been around but not really involved, and yet Deanne still seemed to realize I also needed the friendship of someone my own age.

Yes, there was Max, the boy next door, the guy who'd made my school experience a little less horrible than it otherwise would have been, but because I pretty much had a crush on him from day one, our relationship was a bit more fraught than the friendship I shared with Deanne.

Anyway, there had been no point in trying to hide my feelings about Max from her, and I hadn't bothered to try. Somehow, I'd known she would never tease me about that awful crush, or divulge my secret to anyone. Having my mother abandon me as a baby had given me a whole bunch of trust issues, that was for sure, and yet I knew Deanne would never betray me.

No, the tea leaves hadn't told me that, and neither had I experienced the sort of prophetic dream that might have reinforced my beliefs on the subject of Deanne's trustworthiness. It was more something I felt deep down in my gut, a knowledge that she was the kind of friend who'd stick with me through thick and thin.

Which she had, coming to work with me at the coffee shop after my grandmother died and I was trying to figure out how to run the place on my own. Yes, I'd worked there since high school and knew everything about the business like the back of my hand, but it was still scary to realize the fate of the place now rested on my shoulders, that there wasn't anyone I could really go to for advice.

But I'd survived that rocky transitional period, during which I transformed The Tea Spot into Levitation Latte, making it a true coffee shop rather than a sandwich and coffee and tea kind of place. If anything, business was brisker now than it had ever been, but I doubted I would have been so successful if I hadn't had my best friend there to help me through it all.

"I like that lip gloss," she said, maybe guessing that was a neutral enough topic of conversation that I wouldn't give her the side-eye over it. "Is it new?"

I nodded as I slipped the tube back into the small pouch I'd brought in my tote bag. "Yeah, it's something I found at Walgreens. Physician's Formula...it's called Desert Rose."

"Appropriate," Deanne observed. "And it looks great on you." She paused there, as if wondering whether she should say anything else. Apparently, she decided she might as well plow ahead, because she went on, "He's going to notice one of these days. You've changed so much over the past ten years."

No one could really argue with that particular statement. In high school, I'd been skinny and awkward, nose too big for my face, skin deciding to plague me at the worst possible times, like the day before our school pictures were being taken. As soon as I hit my twenties, though, everything seemed to smooth itself out, my skin finally behaving itself and all my proportions at last becoming much more aesthetically pleasing.

Whether I could compete with the women who shared screen time with Max Sullivan was a subject for some debate, even though I consoled myself that he'd never seemed too interested in dating actresses, had instead opted for those who worked behind the scenes. However, since some of those women were nearly as striking as their on-screen counterparts, I somehow doubted I could be considered real competition for any of them.

"Maybe," I allowed, and then got out a compact and blotted away the shine on my nose. "I'm not going to hold my breath. It's enough that we're friends."

Deanne lifted a brow but didn't bother to contradict me. No doubt she knew the truth of the situation and didn't see any reason to fling it in my face.

"It is nice to have Max back in town," she said diplomatically. "Ready?"

I took one last glance in the mirror. Despite my oh-so-Irish name, I definitely took after my absent mother—big brown eyes, dark hair, a mouth that had once been way too large for my face but had somehow managed to become almost pouty over the years, rather than simply out of proportion.

It would have to do.

"Let's go," I said.

Volunteers working the harvest festival had already assembled our booth, so all Deanne and I had to do was get everything set up—the cookies and muffins placed on various trays, the coffee machines and warming plate for the cider put on a table at the back of the stall and plugged into one of the portable generators that had thoughtfully been arranged at careful intervals behind the line of kiosks. The festival officially started at five, giving us plenty of time to prep and make sure we were ready to go at the assigned hour.

Not that too many people appeared to be taking the official kick-off time very seriously, since there were already small groups roaming around the park, peeking at the wares in the various booths, wandering over to the bandstand where we'd have live music a little bit later in the evening. I knew exactly who was playing, since he'd come in to the shop just the week before to tell me the important news.

"Our first headliner!" Kyle Isaacs had declared, obviously bursting with pride.

At the time, I'd just given him an encouraging smile and told him that was great news, even while hoping he wasn't expecting me to play groupie. Kyle had been a deputy with the Las Vegas police department for the past couple of years, but clearly, he'd never given up his garage band dreams, since he'd been playing with the same group of friends since high school.

He'd also never given up on his dreams of being with me, although we'd broken up almost a year earlier after I'd realized there was basically zero chemistry between us. He didn't appear to have gotten the memo, though, and always seemed to cook up some excuse to come into Levitation Latte and chat me up.

And though my crush on Max Sullivan was a closely guarded secret known only to Deanne and me, it seemed Kyle still wasn't too thrilled about the time I'd spent with my movie star friend, despite it being pretty obvious to everyone that Max was only renewing our childhood acquaintance and nothing more.

Well, I couldn't really blame Kyle for being a bit put off. Having a genuine celebrity as a rival had to be kind of daunting.

To my infinite relief, I didn't see any sign of Kyle as Deanne and I got the booth in order. It seemed likely enough that he was off getting in some last-minute practice with his bandmates, or maybe already setting up at the bandstand. Since it was located on the opposite side of the park from the row of booths where we were currently working, I couldn't really tell what might be going on there.

Despite the golden leaves on the enormous cottonwoods that dotted the park, the afternoon felt mild, promising pretty much perfect weather for the celebration. Once the sun went down, there would be something of a nip in the air, but only enough to make it feel like October, and not the sort of weather where you'd need to really bundle up.

I had a sweater folded in my tote bag for those later, cooler hours, but for the moment, I was just fine in my long-sleeved plaid shirt with the whimsical embroidery around the shoulders and my jeans and flat-soled boots. My hope was that I'd look put together but not as though I was trying too hard.

Not that it probably mattered. As far as I'd been able to tell, Max didn't seem to ever notice what I looked like.

All right, that assessment wasn't entirely fair. When we'd met again after not seeing each other for almost ten years, he actually had commented that I looked great. Unfortunately, there'd been just the slightest hint of surprise in his tone, as though he'd been honestly startled to see I hadn't remained the same gawky girl he remembered.

After that initial compliment, though, he hadn't said a thing about my looks, and I hadn't noticed any particular admiration in his eyes even when I'd done my best to put some effort into my appearance.

Which was fine. I didn't need Max Sullivan's approval.

Yeah, right, I thought.

Around four-thirty, Deanne's husband Mike showed up. He was good-looking in a friendly sort of way, with light brown hair and blue-gray eyes that already had their share of laugh lines around them. He greeted the two of us with a grin, saying, "Reporting for duty!"

"At ease, corporal," I replied with a smile of my own. "You've got about a half hour before you really need to do anything—assuming Max is even on time."

"The movie star doesn't own a watch?" Mike returned, still grinning.

"He owns a very expensive watch," Deanne put in, her expression one of mock severity. "And a very expensive phone. But I'm not sure whether he actually looks at either one of them."

I wished I could argue with that observation, but my friend was right. Max did have a tendency to be late—not so heinously late that you could rake him over the coals for his tardiness, but just enough that he always seemed to be running about fifteen or twenty minutes behind.

"He's probably used to having an assistant tell him where he needs to be," I said mildly, which was only the truth. Max actually did have an assistant back in L.A., but he apparently hadn't seen the need to have her come to Las Vegas. To be fair, they could text and FaceTime and Zoom or whatever, and so it wasn't as though they needed to be in the same room to get things accomplished.

But not having her around meant that Max

had to take care of time management all on his own, and it seemed as though that was a skill he'd lost somewhere over the past ten years. As far as I could remember, he'd always been pretty punctual back in high school. Then again, he'd been living at home, and had his parents to keep him in line.

Mike seemed to understand he should let it go, because he only shrugged and then lifted the plastic cling film that covered one of the trays of cookies, saying, "Mind if snag one?"

"Well, since you've already got your fingers on a snickerdoodle, it's not like I can say no," Deanne remarked, the amused light in her eyes belying her sour tone.

A quick grin as he pulled out the aforementioned cookie and took a large bite. "Mmm," he said. "Skye, you make the best snickerdoodles in three states."

About all I could do was shake my head. "You've eaten snickerdoodles in three states?"

A nod as he bit off another chunk. "They're my favorite, so I try to sample them everywhere I go. And yours are definitely the best in New Mexico, Arizona, and Texas. I'll get back to you on Colorado after I have one there."

Which wouldn't be too far off in the future, since he and Deanne had a trip planned to Denver over the Veteran's Day holiday in November. Luckily, since Denver was just a six-hour trip from Las Vegas, they'd only be gone for three days, two of which would be over the weekend while the coffee shop was closed anyway. I could manage without my friend for one work day, even though I knew it might be a bit of a scramble.

"Sounds like a plan," I said.

Mike carefully folded the cellophane back down over the cookie tray, although, judging by his wistful expression, he was now kicking himself over not grabbing another one while he had the chance. But with Deanne sending him a gimlet stare, he probably figured he'd better quit while he was ahead.

"I'm going to wander around and check out everything," he announced. "Be back in a few."

"A *very* few," Deanne told him. "It'll be five before you know it."

His only answer was a quick lift at the corner of his mouth, and then he headed off along the row of booths, many of which already appeared to be open for business. In fact, we had several people come by and send longing looks at our trays of cookies and muffins, but no one asked to buy any. Deanne and I had agreed that if we started selling stuff early, we'd run out long before the festival was over, so we needed to hold the line for now. I noticed there were already some reporters wandering around, but they seemed more interested in the corn maze than the row of vendors' booths.

After about fifteen minutes, Mike came wandering back, and a little bit after that, I heard a feedback whine from the sound system set up at the bandstand, followed by the sound of Tom Gallegos' voice.

"Welcome, everyone," he said, "to Las Vegas's one hundredth harvest festival!"

A cheer came up from the crowd that had assembled around the bandstand. Over the past couple of minutes, people had been slowly gravitating in that direction, allowing Deanne and me to relax our guard somewhat in terms of protecting the trays of cookies and muffins. And while our position in the vendors' area didn't give us a direct view of the stage, I'd attended enough of these festivals to know pretty much exactly how everything was set up—the mayor standing a little above everyone at the front of the bandstand, with groups of people clustered nearby so they could be there for the event's official kick-off.

"I'm so glad you all came out to celebrate tonight," the mayor continued. "Make sure to visit the vendors at their booths—and you won't want to miss the corn maze, either!"

Another cheer came up, one that sounded a little less loud and maybe somewhat younger. Although I couldn't see who was cheering, I had to guess it was probably a bunch of high school students, eager to use the more secluded parts of the maze for some impromptu make-out sessions.

"And at seven-thirty," the mayor went on, "we have our very own Pecos Pride playing a set right here at the bandstand, something you won't want to miss!"

The crowd cheered again, although this response was even more subdued than the last. Kyle's band was decent, but I had a feeling its country-flavored rock wasn't exactly the sort of thing most high school kids cared too much about.

"But that's enough from me," Tom concluded, although I kind of got the impression he wouldn't have minded talking for at least five minutes more. "Go on and enjoy the festival!"

Everyone clapped, and that appeared to be the end of the kick-off ceremonies, because people immediately began streaming toward the booths, intent on some hardcore snacking...or a real meal, since a food truck from one of my favorite local restaurants, The Skillet, was also on hand to serve some of their amazing tacos. In fact, I'd already made a mental note to slip by with Max at some point so we could have something more substantial to eat than cookies and kettle corn.

The Levitation Latte booth was overwhelmed for the next few minutes as people scooped up muffins and cookies and cups of pumpkin spice latte or spiced cider to wash down their treats. Right then, I was glad Deanne and I had Mike to help out, because the crowd felt even bigger than it had in previous years.

Maybe the newly expanded corn maze had turned out to be more of a draw than I'd thought.

Eventually, though, the throng ebbed a bit, just enough for me to catch my breath. Good thing, too, because in the next moment, I caught a glimpse of Max making his way through the crowd, looking as godlike as ever, like some heavenly being who'd deigned to descend from Olympus to mingle with us mere mortals.

Okay, that was probably a silly thing to think, considering he was a local just like the rest of us, but still, I had to admit he was looking pretty awesome that evening, in a weathered leather jacket over a dark blue T-shirt, faded jeans, and scuffed boots that appeared as though he'd broken them in by wandering the back forty on his ranch. Since the place comprised more than a hundred acres, that was a lot of back forty to cover. His golden brown hair caught the light of the setting sun, and it seemed as though he stood a head taller than most of the crowd, although that impression could have merely been due to his confident stride.

"Hey," he said as he approached the booth. "Sorry I'm late."

Mike and Deanne exchanged a loaded glance,

but to my relief, neither of them said anything except "hi" in response.

"It's fine," I said quickly. "All you really missed was the mayor's kick-off speech."

Max's blue eyes glinted, bright in the light of a sun that was just beginning to slip behind the Sangre de Cristo mountains to the west. "Yeah, that's probably something I can live without."

"So, are you going straight to the corn maze, or are you going to shop first?" Deanne asked. Her mouth had that twitch to it that told me she was doing her best to hold back a grin...and which also told me she'd probably been thinking the same thing about the corn maze I had.

As much as I would have loved to have Max pull me into a secret corner of the maze and declare his undying love for me, I somehow doubted that was going to happen. "Whatever Max wants to do," I said.

He glanced down the row of booths. "We might as well wander around here first, don't you think?"

"Sounds like a great idea," I replied, and slipped out from behind the table that held all our cookies and muffins. "You two hold down the fort."

"On it," Mike said. He, too, looked as though he was doing his best to stifle a smile.

Time to get out of here before one of them said something I regretted. "Let's go look at the soap," I told Max as I came over and stood next to him. "I've been wanting to get some for a while—there's nothing better than Anna Ortega's goat milk stuff."

This suggestion seemed to be just fine with Max, because he only nodded and said, "Sure."

We wandered away from the Levitation Latte booth as I did my best to contain a shiver of anticipation. Maybe we were doing this as friends and nothing more, but still, I was walking through the harvest festival with Max Sullivan at my side.

I couldn't wait to see what happened next.

CHAPTER 3

Bitter Harvest

Well, not a whole lot happened at first. Max dutifully trailed after me as I went from booth to booth, buying soap here and a carved wooden hair stick there. In the background, I actually did catch a glimpse of Max's bodyguard, Lou D'Amato, lurking at a safe distance, but since he clearly seemed to be doing his best to be unobtrusive, I decided I wouldn't comment on his presence. There was absolutely nothing to indicate that Max and I weren't safe here, and yet I could see why he'd want to be careful, considering someone had tried to frame him for murder only the month before.

Just as I was about to suggest that we head over to The Skillet's food truck for tacos, however, I found our path blocked by just about the last person I wanted to see.

Raylene Bryant.

She definitely looked much better than the time I'd caught a glimpse of her at Max's arraignment, maybe ten pounds or even more lighter, the brassiness in her hair toned down and her makeup expertly applied. No sign of her kids, and I wondered if she'd used some of her trust money to hire a babysitter to watch them for the evening, or whether they were merely preoccupied by the bouncy castle at the end of the row of booths.

"Hi, Max," she said brightly with a sideways glance toward me, so dismissive I could feel angry blood begin to rise in my cheeks.

Maybe Max noticed, or maybe he didn't. Either way, his tone was friendly but at the same time almost too casual as he replied, "Hi, Raylene. How've you been? And the kids?"

"Oh, we're all fine," she said. "They're playing in the bouncy castle with some friends, so I thought I'd wander around a little."

Well, that confirmed my suspicions as to where her children were, but since the youngest was barely four, I thought that was a bit young for them to be left mostly unattended.

Since one corner of Max's mouth tightened a little, it seemed as though much the same thought had just passed through his head.

"And you?" she asked, acting as though I wasn't standing right there.

"Oh, Skye and I are just making the rounds," he said, making sure he emphasized my name in his reply. "She was nice enough to agree to be my tour guide."

I wanted to hug him for making that statement, for making it sound as though I was doing him a favor by being his companion at the festival. Naturally, I wouldn't do anything as crazy as throw my arms around him in such a public place...and especially in front of Raylene...but his comment warmed my heart nonetheless.

She clearly wasn't thrilled by the remark, because her mouth tightened for a second before she said, voice too sticky-sweet, "Yes, I suppose that was nice of her...not that she has much else to do with her spare time."

What a—

"Well, it was nice seeing you, Raylene," Max said, his tone now clearly dismissive. "Have a good evening."

And he looped his arm through mine and gently tugged me away.

Just that little bit of contact was enough to send a thrill through my entire body, but I knew I needed to act cool, that he was just doing what he had to in order to put some space between the two of us and his unwelcome ex-girlfriend.

"Talk about someone who hasn't improved

with age," he grumbled once we were safely out of earshot.

"Well, she's been dealing with a lot lately," I said, figuring I could be magnanimous since it was painfully clear whose side Max was on.

He paused then, stopping a few yards away from The Skillet's food truck. People were lined up to place their orders and thankfully didn't seem to be paying much attention to the two of us, despite Max's movie star status. Clearly, hunger trumped celebrities in their minds.

"You don't have to stick up for Raylene," he said, expression almost annoyed...but not quite.

It took a lot to irritate Max Sullivan.

"I'm not sticking up for her," I replied at once, then amended, "All right, maybe I am...a little bit. But she's going through all this with three kids to manage, and she probably feels overwhelmed now that her husband isn't around."

"A husband she's divorcing," Max pointed out. "A guy she was willing to dump at the slightest hint from me."

Okay, all that was true enough. The whole reason why Evan Bryant had been so pissed off at Max in the first place was that he'd discovered how Raylene had been writing to her celebrity former boyfriend, telling him she was willing to leave her husband and the kids behind if only he'd give the word.

I'd never condone murder, let alone trying to frame someone for it, but on the other hand, it wasn't as though the crime had been entirely without motive...if only in Evan's angry and jealous mind.

A lift of my shoulders, and then I said, "But you set up that trust fund for her kids."

"Because they're the innocent victims in all this," he responded at once. "Their parents may be hot messes, but it doesn't mean their lives should go down the toilet because of that. Besides, it's not like I can't afford it."

Again, true. While Max hadn't exactly publicized the amount of money he'd put in the trust, rumors swirled that it was three million dollars, a million for each of Evan and Raylene's kids. That seemed like an unholy chunk of money, but considering he was getting paid five times that for the action-adventure flick he'd be filming in January, it wasn't something he'd probably miss too much.

"Still," I said. "I don't know how many people would have done the same thing."

Now his expression brightened, and he flashed me one of his patented Max Sullivan million-dollar smiles. "Well, I'm not 'most people.' Now, let's go get some tacos."

We did exactly that, fortifying ourselves with barbacoa and carnitas and grilled chicken versions, and then brought some back to the Levitation Latte booth to feed the troops there. Mike and Deanne looked as though they'd been busy, since the trays of muffins and cookies were noticeably depleted.

However, she immediately brushed off my offer to spell her for a while so she and her husband could do some wandering of their own. "I mean, it's the same people who've been here year after year," she told me around bites of a chicken taco. "We'll want to go visit the corn maze after you and Max have checked it out, but nothing else is new for us the way it is for him."

"I appreciate that," he said at once, then took a bite of his own taco. His expression might have been the slightest bit wistful, and I got the feeling he was wishing he had a beer or a margarita to wash it down. Unfortunately for him, the Las Vegas harvest festival was a dry event, so he'd have to wait until he got home to indulge that urge.

Well, unless he invited me to the bar at the Plaza Hotel after we were done at the festival. It was conveniently located only steps away...and the bar stayed open until ten o'clock.

I mentally crossed my fingers but didn't say anything out loud, figuring if it happened, it happened.

We had to break off the conversation there for a bit, since a family came by and got hot cider for their kids and pumpkin spice lattes for the adults, along with nearly the last of the snickerdoodles. As soon as the little group was gone, Max pounced.

"I'll take two of the snickerdoodles," he said. "Don't want to miss out on those."

I smiled a bit as Deanne popped them into a paper bag and handed them over, and he gave her a five-dollar bill. The cookies were actually only a dollar a piece, but I guessed she wouldn't bother to make any change. He would only have refused it, anyway.

Sure enough, she slid the bill into the pocket of her apron and said, obviously doing her best to ignore Mike's woebegone expression as he watched the last of his beloved snickerdoodles get spirited away, "Enjoy them."

"Oh, I will," Max replied.

We walked away from the booth, heading across the park to the corn maze. As we went, I said, "You know I'd be happy to bake you an entire batch of snickerdoodles."

He slid one out of the bag and took a bite. "I know you would," he said after he'd swallowed the mouthful of cookie. "But I wanted one now, and it's all for a good cause, right?"

I supposed he had a point there, as twenty-five percent of all the proceeds from the booths at the festival would be donated to the Las Vegas Historical Society's preservation fund, and used to keep our little town's vintage buildings in tip-top shape. "Right," I replied, then added, "But my offer of a batch of cookies still stands."

"And I'll definitely take you up on that whenever you have a chance to whip some up," Max said. "Only better make it a double batch, since I know I'll have to share with Lou and Al."

"Maybe a triple batch," I returned with a grin. It was so like Max to ask for extra cookies...and also like him to make sure he shared with his bodyguards.

One of whom was about fifteen or so paces behind us, far enough back that he couldn't eavesdrop on what we were saying, but close enough that he could definitely tackle anyone who tried to get too close to his boss. I had to wonder what Lou thought of all this, whether he considered us hopelessly provincial, or whether he thought his current gig was a nice break from life in the big city. Because decent rental properties were in short supply in Las Vegas, Max had actually bought both Al and Lou houses here in town, nice little two-bedroom properties that had been recently fixed up and which would probably earn their new owners a decent profit when the time came to head back to Albuquerque.

Or maybe they planned to stay here indefinitely, and would travel with him whenever he went off to shoot a movie. I knew the one Max had scheduled for January was supposed to be filming in Costa Rica part of the time, which I had to admit sounded like a nice break from northern New Mexico's often snowy winters.

We came to the corn maze, which was illuminated by some portable lights, the sort of thing you might find at a carnival or in the parking lot at a football field so people could tailgate comfortably. I hadn't really been paying much attention, but I realized that way more than an hour had passed since the mayor made his speech, and it was now almost full dark. Despite the lighting, there were still pockets of shadow where the maze twisted and turned, and I found myself gladder than ever that I'd have Max as my companion as we made our way through the attraction.

He handed over a twenty-dollar bill to the high school girl who was watching the entrance and collecting admission. Wide-eyed and obviously star-struck, she started digging in the pouch she wore around her belt to make change, but he stopped her, saying, "Oh, keep it."

"All for a good cause," I piped up, and he smiled.

"Exactly."

After that exchange, we made our way into the maze, really just bales of hay set up in twisting patterns, the walls of hay decorated with stalks of dried corn. Quiet footsteps behind us told me that Lou was bringing up the rear, but because of the way we kept winding around, following the maze's complicated corridors, I couldn't actually see him.

We walked in silence for a few moments, and then Max said, "So...read any good tea leaves lately?"

I shot an arch glance up at him. "Need your fortune read?"

That question got me a head shake, although his expression was amused. "No, I think I'm good for now. At least, I don't see any immediate bumps in the road, unless someone else decides to frame me for murder."

"I haven't had any prophetic dreams on that front lately," I told him. "So I think you're probably safe. Anyway, I've done a few readings for my regulars, but none of them were exactly what you could call earthshaking. On the upside, I did manage to convince Ivy Mulaney that it wasn't a good idea to send her entire Social Security check to that televangelist she watches every Sunday."

"Definitely a good deed," Max agreed.

Now I couldn't help smiling. "Yep...especially since he was charged with fraud and embezzlement only two days after the reading I did for Mrs. Mulaney. She called and thanked me, and told me she was going to stick with what she puts in the collection plate at her church from now on."

"Good call," he said, and then shook his head slightly as we rounded another turn in the maze. The breeze had picked up as the sun went down behind the mountains, but in here it felt warmer, the air filled with the dry, rich scent of hay. Another hesitation, and then he added, "Have you ever thought about doing something more?"

"'Something more'?" I repeated, not sure what my friend was driving at.

"With your talent," he clarified. "It seems to me you have a true gift. You should be doing something more with it than reading tea leaves for little old ladies who get scammed by TV preachers."

I shrugged. "What else am I supposed to do? Contact a cable channel and see if they want to produce a show about a Las Vegas medium?"

Never mind that I wasn't a medium at all. I didn't talk to ghosts or channel spirits from other planes or whatever. No, I just read tea leaves, and had the oddly prophetic dream from time to time. Neither of those was the sort of talent that exactly made for compelling television, even if I were the sort of person who would have been comfortable on camera, which I most definitely was not.

However, Max obviously didn't have the same reservations about my supposed talents that I did. "Why not? It would be cool."

"No, it wouldn't," I returned at once. "I'm not into that kind of thing. I don't want to be famous."

"You don't?" he asked, looking genuinely surprised. "Why not?"

"Are you forgetting my brush with the paparazzi?" I replied. Since it had only been a month earlier when I was getting followed by a skeevy guy with an oversized camera who was desperately hoping to dig up something salacious going on between Max and me, I had a hard time believing the incident could have slipped his mind.

Which it obviously hadn't, because now he grinned down at me, smile bright as ever even though the day had darkened into twilight. "Oh, that was nothing."

"It wasn't 'nothing' to me," I said. "Anyway, I don't want to live my life like that." I stopped, and Max paused next to me, his gaze now earnest, as though I'd just revealed a component of my personality he'd never before seen. "I know it's probably old hat to you, but even you said you liked being here in Las Vegas because it helps you avoid a lot of that crap."

"Okay, that's true enough," he responded. "I mean, it's nice to get a break from the b.s. every once in a while. But paparazzi aren't enough to make me want to give up all the rest of it."

"I can see that," I said, glad that he hadn't tried to keep pushing me on the subject. Some people might have said Max Sullivan wasn't exactly the most perceptive person in the world, since he was definitely the type to charge in first and think later. However, he wouldn't be as good an actor as he was if he didn't also have good instincts about people, about what made them tick. "Besides," I went on, "everyone knew you were destined for greatness, Max. If anyone from West Las Vegas High School was going to make it big, it was you."

Being Max, he didn't even blink at that statement. "Now you're going to give me a big head."

"Too late," I said, and he placed a mock-punch on my nearest bicep, just like he would have back when we were little kids and I'd teased him for one thing or another.

"Thanks," he replied, but since he was smiling, I knew he hadn't taken offense at my comment. Then his expression sobered slightly, and he went on, "But seriously—what do you *really* want from all this?"

And he gestured toward the high hay-bale walls of the maze around us, although I guessed he meant all of Las Vegas, not just the park we currently occupied.

"I've got everything I want," I said, which mostly the truth. The one piece of the puzzle that remained was the man who stood next to me, although I knew I'd never have the guts to tell him that particular truth.

"You're serious."

"Yeah," I said, and then tilted my head at him. "Why would you think I wasn't?"

His shoulders lifted. "I suppose it's because I've spent the past ten years surrounded by people who were always looking to get ahead, always trying to be the next big thing. I don't think I ever heard a single person say they were happy with where they were."

Considering what I'd heard about life in Hollywood, this revelation wasn't terribly surprising. At the same time, I reflected there was something to be said for living life in the slow lane. "Well, that's sad," I remarked.

For a moment or two, Max was silent. Then his head tilted just a bit as he took a glance around us, and he replied, "Yeah, I guess it kind of is." He went quiet again when we moved forward a few more paces, then said, "All the same, I think you should do more to develop your talent. I've never met anyone else with your kind of gifts, which tells me they're the sort of thing that should be cultivated. It's like...." The words trailed off as he appeared to consider what he wanted to say next. When he spoke again, his voice was emphatic. "It's like a kid who can play a Mozart sonata by ear deciding he doesn't want piano lessons."

That particular analogy made me smile. "If the

kid can play Mozart by ear, then what does he need with lessons?"

Max didn't return my smile. "You know what I mean. No matter how strong your talent might be, there's still always a way to develop it further."

Tone light, I remarked, "Well, if you know someone who's giving psychic lessons, send them on over."

Now his mouth did lift a bit. "Okay, psychic teachers are probably in short supply. But there's no reason why you can't practice on your own. That's the only way to get better."

I didn't reply at once, mostly because I'd thought the same thing on more than one occasion, wondering whether I might get better at what I did if I just worked a little harder at it. On the other hand, I hadn't really seen any need to. Reading tea leaves was just something I did on the side. Running Levitation Latte was my real mission in life.

Or...was it? I'd told Max I was perfectly happy where I was, but was that the whole truth? Did I really have no other ambition than to run a coffee shop in a small town that most people had never heard of?

And since I didn't know whether I was ready to answer those questions yet, I picked up my pace, thinking the sooner we got out of this corn maze, the sooner I could get back to the booth and away from these troublesome questions. I didn't want to examine my life. I wanted everything to carry on just as it always had.

Correctly gauging my mood, Max didn't say anything else, only began walking a little faster as well, his strides neatly matching mine.

Because we were moving quickly, we almost tripped over the body. At the last minute, Max grabbed my arm, hauling me back before I went sprawling over the figure that lay prone on the ground in front of us.

My free hand went to my mouth as I realized what—I mean, who—was blocking the path through the corn maze.

Mayor Gallegos lay there, eyes staring sightlessly up at the trees overhead, a rope knotted around his neck.

CHAPTER 4

Tough Questions

I sat on a hay bale, blinking my eyes against the flashing blue and red lights of the squad cars clustered near the curb a few yards away. From what I could tell, it looked as though every cop in Las Vegas had descended on Plaza Park following Max's and my discovery of the mayor's body.

Max stood right behind me, while Deanne and Mike hovered off to one side. She'd brought me a pumpkin spice latte for fortification, although right then I could only think of Max's former co-star, Lauralee Peters, who'd doctored her coffee with brandy following the murder of her director...and lover.

Right then, I completely understood the urge to add something a little more bracing to my beverage.

But that would have to wait. At the moment, I had a much more pressing claim on my time.

Chief Maria DeVargas eyed both Max and me as she lifted her notepad. She was a tall woman in her late forties who managed to make even her khaki police uniform look elegant. "And neither of you saw anything?"

"Nothing," Max responded immediately, since of course the police chief had asked her question while I was in the middle of taking a sip of latte. "We were just walking along and talking, and we practically tripped over the guy."

I winced.

"Over Mayor Gallegos," Max amended, apparently realizing his comment hadn't sounded very respectful.

However, Chief DeVargas didn't seem taken aback by his unfortunate choice of words. She made a few notes, then asked, "Did you hear anything that sounded like a struggle?"

This time, I was the one who answered. "No," I told her. "I mean, like Max said, we were talking and weren't paying a whole lot of attention to our surroundings, but I have to believe that if Mayor Gallegos was struggling with someone or having a fight of some kind, we would have heard it."

And even if we hadn't, something like that would've quickly drawn the attention of Max's bodyguard Lou. He'd actually been the one to call the police, his cell phone off his belt and at his ear while Max and I were still gaping down at the corpse.

The response had been almost instantaneous; the police station was right across the street from the park's west side, and besides, there had been plenty of cops on duty that evening, making sure no fights broke out or that no one had decided to slip behind a tree and spark up a joint. Pot was legal in New Mexico, but you couldn't smoke it in a public place like Plaza Park.

One person who wasn't on duty was poor Kyle Isaacs. He stood with some of his fellow deputies a few paces away, looking completely out of place in his ripped jeans and black cowboy shirt and boots. His outfit for the set his band was supposed to play tonight, a set that would never get performed, thanks to the tragedy that had interrupted the town's centennial harvest festival.

Beyond the deputies were clumps of onlookers who murmured amongst themselves but who clearly had been told they needed to stay back and out of the way.

Chief DeVargas made a few more notes. If the set of her mouth was any indication, she wasn't too thrilled by the lack of useful information Max and I were providing.

Well, I wished we could tell her more, but there simply wasn't anything else to say. I couldn't call myself an expert or anything, but that brief glimpse I'd gotten of the mayor's stricken face as Max and Lou hustled me away made me think he must have been dead for some time before we literally stumbled across him. The man's usually warm brown complexion had looked slack and pale, as though enough time had passed to allow the blood to drain away.

Which meant...what? That he'd been murdered almost as soon as he stepped off the stage after giving his little welcoming speech at the beginning of the festival?

It felt that way to me, even if I didn't have any real evidence to back up my theory. I supposed the medical examiner's office would figure it out soon enough.

"Was there anyone else nearby?" the chief asked next, and almost in unison, Max and I shook our heads.

"No," Max said. "Lou, my bodyguard"—he stopped to incline his head in the man's direction —"wasn't too far behind us, but we didn't see anyone else from the time we stepped into the maze to the moment when we encountered Mayor Gallegos' body."

"And you didn't think that was strange?" she returned.

Max and I exchanged a glance. Put that way, it did seem a little weird that the two of us had been afforded so much privacy during our stroll through the corn maze. I supposed at the time I'd just figured most of the kids had already gone through it and moved on to other diversions, since we hadn't wandered that way until after it had already been open for almost two hours.

"Not really," he said smoothly. "I mean, I can't speak for whoever might have been ahead of us, but I'd asked Lou to make sure no one would come up too close behind Skye and me."

I hadn't known about that. Most likely, Max had made the request of his bodyguard before they even got to the park. While I would have liked to think he'd asked for a buffer zone because he wanted to make sure any intimacies with me wouldn't be interrupted, it was probably more that he simply wanted to ensure that his privacy was maintained and he wouldn't have to worry about fans bumping into us and asking for selfies, or whatever.

The chief made a few more notes, her quietly steely expression another indication that she was less than thrilled by the apparent lack of any useful clues regarding the mayor's murder. Whoever had done it obviously must have had nerves of steel to kill a man in such a public place and then leave his body lying where they clearly wanted it to be found.

Or maybe he hadn't been killed at the park at

all. Maybe he'd been murdered someplace else and then dumped here as a way of throwing the police off the scent.

Despite managing to solve the mystery of Perry Lockhart's death, I certainly wasn't anyone who could begin to puzzle out how such a thing might have happened. You would think that one of the attendees at the festival surely must have noticed someone carrying a dead body across the park, but maybe poor Tom Gallegos had been disguised somehow.

"Well, thank you for your input," Chief DeVargas said. She didn't sound particularly grateful, but that was probably because she knew she was looking forward to a long investigation with this particular crime. So far, the evidence definitely didn't indicate an open-and-shut case. "You can go now. Someone from the police department will contact you if we need any additional information."

"Sorry we couldn't be more help," Max said, and she gave him a thin-lipped smile.

"Not your fault," she replied briefly before turning away from us so she could have some kind of murmured convo with the deputies who'd been standing back and watching the entire exchange.

Deanne stepped forward as soon as it was clear the chief didn't have anything further to say to us. "Oh, my God," she said. "Are you guys all right?"

"We're fine," I replied quickly, then looked up at Max. "I mean...I think we are?"

"Sure," he said, tone as easy as though we were all chatting at a backyard barbecue or something, rather than a few yards away from the scene of a crime. "Not gonna lie—it was kind of a shock, but obviously, neither Skye nor I had anything to do with what happened to the mayor, so...."

"So I think I just want to go home and get some rest," I finished for him. I sent a pleading look at Deanne and her husband, who stood just behind her. "Do you guys mind too much if you pack up the booth? If not, I can help, but—"

"No, you've had a shock," she broke in at once, clearly needing to let me know she had no intention of allowing me to clean up the Levitation Latte food stand. "Honestly, there isn't that much left, anyway. We're totally cleaned out of baked goods, so all Mike and I have to do is pack up the beverage stuff and take it over to the shop. It's fine."

"Thanks," I said, and hoped she could hear the gratitude in that single syllable.

"Let me drive you home," Max said.

I sent him a weary smile. "My car's behind the shop."

"Leave it there," he told me. "I'll drive you over to get it tomorrow morning after we have breakfast."

"'Breakfast'?" I repeated blankly.

"Yes, breakfast," he said. "We can go to Charlie's. My treat."

Who was I to turn down a breakfast invitation from Max Sullivan...even if I might have preferred that said breakfast had been preceded by a night spent together?

"Sounds great," I said.

———————

Max drove me home in his shiny new black Bronco —not the rental he'd been driving when he first came to town, but a vehicle he'd bought recently once he knew he was going to be hanging around Las Vegas for the foreseeable future. I leaned my head against the back of the seat and inhaled the welcoming aroma of new leather, gladder than I'd thought I would be that I didn't have to be the one behind the wheel.

Who knew the death of someone who was at best an acquaintance could be so draining?

True, as Deanne had said, I'd had a pretty big shock. This wasn't like Perry Lockhart's death, which I'd only heard about secondhand. I hadn't seen his body...hadn't heard him speaking only a few hours before he died.

One thought kept circling around and around in my mind.

Who would want Tom Gallegos dead?

No one I could think of. The guy could be annoying sometimes, but if every irritating person on the face of the planet was targeted for death, the world's population would probably drop by at least half overnight. And being the mayor, he'd tussled with a few of the locals, like Noah Matthews, who'd been fighting city hall over an easement on his property for at least the past five years, or Tina Jacobs, who wanted her neighborhood rezoned so she could operate a nail salon out of her house.

Were any of the grudges those people harbored against the mayor sufficient to result in murder? I didn't want to think so, but then again, before a month ago, I wouldn't have thought Evan Bryant was capable of killing a man in cold blood, either.

Max parked the Bronco in front of my place, a carefully restored farmhouse-style home that, like the harvest festival itself, was now entering its second century. We got out of the SUV and walked up the front steps, then crossed the porch so I could unlock the front door and let us in.

After I closed the door and locked it again, Max let out a breath. "Hell of a night."

"That's for sure," I said. The half a pumpkin spice latte I'd just drunk had made me feel a little zingy, and I wanted to tone things down. "Glass of wine?" I suggested.

He grinned. "Thought you'd never ask."

I sent him an answering smile. "Go ahead and make yourself comfortable—I'll get us a couple of glasses of chardonnay. Is that all right?"

"Sounds great."

Feeling relieved, I headed into the kitchen. I'd opened the bottle the night before so I could have a glass with the grilled chicken salad I'd had for dinner, and the thrifty part of me hadn't wanted to open a second one just to serve to my unexpected guest. Luckily, it seemed as though Max was only looking for a muscle relaxant and didn't much care which form it took.

Probably, brandy or whisky or something along those lines would have been even better, but I didn't drink hard liquor and so didn't have any on hand. Around the holidays, I'd make my grandmother's famous high-octane rum balls and would have some leftover rum I might use for occasions like this one, but I hadn't even thought about gathering the ingredients for the holiday treats quite yet.

A glass in each hand, I returned to the living room. Max had sat down on the couch, so I settled myself in one of the wing chairs that faced the sofa across a coffee table. While I would have loved to take a seat next to him, I knew I wasn't brave enough for that kind of maneuver.

His expression was thoughtful, as if he'd been pondering Tom Gallegos' demise while I was out of the room. He took the glass I handed him and said, "Thanks," before swallowing some of the chardonnay.

Obviously, he wasn't in a toasting mood tonight...not that I could blame him. What would we have toasted, anyway? That at least this time around there wasn't much chance of being suspects in a murder?

Cold comfort, but I'd take it. I also swallowed some chardonnay and immediately felt a little better. Not all the way, but my nerves did seem as though they were starting to settle down.

"Who would've wanted to kill the mayor?" Max asked abruptly. "And why?"

About all I could do was give a helpless lift of my shoulders. "I have absolutely no idea," I replied, then figured I'd better elaborate somewhat, since I'd been pondering possible suspects on the way over here. "I mean, I suppose it's possible Tom Gallegos collected a few enemies along the way, since he was just starting his second term and has been in public office for a while, and there are some people around here who aren't super happy with all his decisions. On the other hand, I don't think I've ever heard anyone complain enough about anything he did that it would end up in murder. Trying to vote him out, sure."

Max leaned forward on the sofa, bright blue gaze intent, almost eager. "Like who?"

I'd already shrugged, so I just gave a slight wave of the hand holding my wine glass before I lifted it to my lips and took another sip. My suspicions had been so vague, I didn't think it was a good idea to mention them now. "I don't know," I said, then added as an idea struck me, "I think some of the people in those ranchettes off Cinder Road got kind of pissed off at him for allowing the zoning to get changed in one of the lots at the far end so they could build a gas station there."

That comment got me a lifted brow. "Angry enough they'd want him dead?"

At once, I shook my head. "I doubt it. They were bitching and moaning all the way until it opened...and then they realized they wouldn't have to drive as far to fill up their cars or even to grab a few snacks, since the gas station also has a convenience store. I'm pretty sure that theory is a dead end."

Max didn't appear too put off by my reply, because he only seemed to consider those words for a moment before he said, "Well, maybe it was a crime of passion."

Somehow, I couldn't imagine Tom Gallegos being the object of someone's unrequited lust. He wasn't a bad-looking guy, but his hair had started to thin and he'd definitely slid into dad-bod territory the past couple of years. "I doubt it," I replied.

"As far as I know, he's been happily married for more than ten years."

"That's no indicator," Max responded at once. Clearly, he wasn't about to let any of this go. "Maybe it's someone he worked with. Does he have an assistant?"

"Cory?" I said, knowing how dubious I must have sounded.

"Cory Sills?" Max didn't wait for me to answer, though, and only went on, "She was a year ahead of me, but I knew her because we were in drama together. She also seemed kind of intense...just the sort of person who might take matters into her own hands if she didn't get her way."

About all I could do was let out an uneasy chuckle at that outlandish suggestion. "Max, have you been watching *telenovelas* or something in your spare time?"

Now he did crack a smile. "No," he said. "Believe it or not, I've been doing a lot of work in the garden, getting things ready for winter. It sort of helps me feel like the place is really mine."

Well, there went my theory about him hiring a gardener to take care of the ranch house's extensive grounds. "I never got even the slightest hint that Cory felt anything for Tom Gallegos except what any person might feel for a guy who's her boss," I said. "Anyway, even if I were going to accept the slightly crazy notion that Cory had some kind of motive for killing the mayor, how would she even have managed something like that? The guy was obviously throttled with a rope and left there, something that would require a lot of strength. She's just not physically up to that sort of thing."

Which was only the truth. I was only a modest five foot five, and Cory had to be at least an inch and a half shorter than me and probably weighed no more than a hundred and fifteen pounds wringing wet. There was no way in the world she would have been able to haul two hundred pounds of dead weight into that corn maze without someone else noticing.

"Maybe she had an accomplice," Max suggested.

"I'd say that was a pretty long shot," I said, then paused. "Really, I don't have any theories. I think we should just let Chief DeVargas handle this."

A pained expression crossed his face. "Because she did such a good job figuring out who killed Perry Lockhart."

All right, he had a point there. Still, I had to believe Marie DeVargas would have tracked down Perry Lockhart's murderer at some point, if only because I had a feeling that Shawn Zales eventually would have succumbed to guilt and told the police about his friend Evan's request to access the storage unit where the movie's props—including the portable gun safe that contained the murder weapon—were being kept.

I sipped some chardonnay before replying, "This is entirely different. Anyway, we're not involved in this case."

"Except for tripping over Tom Gallegos' body," Max pointed out. His blue eyes narrowed, and he added, "What if someone left his body there exactly because they wanted us to find it?"

Apparently, my friend had an unlimited supply of crazy theories. I wanted to tell him this wasn't the movies and real life usually didn't work that way, but I refrained from stating my opinion quite so bluntly. Instead, I replied, "I suppose that's remotely possible, but I don't really see how someone could coordinate a plot like that. I mean, it's not as though we had a set time when we were going into the maze, something we'd announced to everyone. We just sort of wandered over there after we were done eating our tacos."

His expression fell, and I got the impression he hadn't considered that angle. However, since this was Max Sullivan, it wasn't as though he intended to give up quite so easily. "But you're still going to look into it, aren't you? Brew up some tea leaves and see what they tell you?"

I should have told him that of course I wasn't going to do a tea-leaf reading on the subject, that I was going to leave the matter to the police. We'd given our statement, and that should have been the end of it.

But because my spirit was definitely weak when it came to Max, I only said, "Well, I can try. I can't promise you anything, though. This is an entirely different situation from the last time someone was killed in Las Vegas."

Those words didn't seem to discourage him...in fact, just the opposite. His eyes lit up, and he said, "I know you'll figure it out. Why wait for Chief DeVargas to solve the mystery when you can use the leaves to give you all the answers you need?"

I sent him a watery smile. As I took another sip of chardonnay, I hoped I wasn't getting myself into something I couldn't easily get out of...and feared that was exactly what I was doing.

CHAPTER 5

Tea and Sympathy

"You know he just wants to play Hardy Boys with you because he's bored," Deanne told me the next morning when she called to see how I was doing. We didn't have a lot of time to talk because Max was picking me up at ten, but since he was almost always a little late, I figured I could squeeze in some conversation before I had to go.

Since that same thought about Max amusing himself playing detective had passed through my head after I'd said goodbye to him the night before —and after he'd confirmed our breakfast "date"—I didn't bother to argue with her. "Oh, I know," I said. "And I have no intention of doing any real meddling. But I figure I can brew some tea this afternoon and see if the leaves have anything to say. Honestly, I'm not expecting much, but at least then I can tell Max I tried."

She made a noncommittal sound. "I guess you know what you're doing," she replied, although the dubious note in her voice indicated she thought pretty much the exact opposite.

"Like I said, I'm not going to get in the way," I assured her. "The last time...that was different. That was about making sure Max didn't go to prison for a crime he didn't commit. I'm not really involved this time around. It's horrible what happened to the mayor, but it's not like he was my best friend or a member of my family or something."

For a few seconds, Deanne was quiet. Then she said, "Well, okay. But still...be careful. You know Max has a talent for dragging people into things they might otherwise have avoided."

That he did. It was probably because his enthusiasm was so infectious that you ended up going along with him, only to realize after it was too late that you were in way over your head. This wasn't so awful when you were only talking about high school pranks, like some of the innocent mischief he used to get up to with his football buddies, but I had the idea that Chief DeVargas would take a pretty dim view of a civilian like me poking her nose in where it didn't belong.

In the aftermath of Evan Bryant's arrest, I'd been pretty vague about what had made me go talk to his friend Shawn Zales in the first place, only saying I'd gotten a hinky feeling when someone mentioned that Evan's father owned the storage facility where the *Perdition Road* crew had been keeping their props. Most people in town knew I read tea leaves and sometimes had dreams that were just a little too accurate, so I had to believe the police chief was in possession of that same information. To my infinite relief, though, she hadn't pushed me on the topic, but had only said I should have come to the police with my suspicions and that I could have gotten myself in a lot of trouble.

A remark I couldn't really argue with, considering the way Evan had shown up at my house, armed and looking for revenge after Shawn had told him I was poking around where I shouldn't.

"I'm not going to do anything risky," I assured Deanne again. "Really, I doubt the tea leaves are going to show me much of anything. And I also doubt I'll have any dreams about the mayor's murder, either, because it's not like he was someone I was close to."

Again, no more than the truth. I'd known him the same way I knew a lot of people in town, because they came into Levitation Latte to get coffee or a muffin or whatever. It wasn't like we'd been besties. And while the tea leaves seemed to work for just about anyone who asked me to read them, the dreams were different. Those only seemed to involve people I was truly close to.

"Well, that's good," Deanne said, then amended quickly, "I mean, just that this isn't the kind of situation where your dreams would be of much use."

The doorbell rang then, and I said, "Sounds like Max is here. I'll talk to you later."

She immediately responded, "Tell him I said hi —and let me know all the juicy details of your breakfast date."

I highly doubted there would be anything "juicy" about a breakfast get-together that was anything but a date. However, I still told her of course I would, then ended the call and shoved the phone into my purse, which was sitting on the coffee table. A few quick steps to the door—I'd been sitting in the living room as I talked to Deanne, figuring I shouldn't be too far away in case Max actually showed up on time—and I opened it and smiled at him. "Morning!"

Was that greeting too chirpy, considering we'd stumbled across a dead body only the night before?

Apparently not, because Max smiled down at me and responded, "Morning! Ready to go?"

"Just let me get my purse."

Once it was slung over my shoulder and I'd locked the front door behind me, we headed down the porch steps to get into his Bronco.

"So, any news from the tea leaves?" he asked

once we'd fastened our seatbelts and he'd pulled away from the curb.

"Oh, it's way too early for that," I replied, which wasn't a complete lie. For whatever reason, it usually felt better for me to read leaves in the afternoon or early evening. Maybe it was only that I was better able to justify such an activity once I'd gotten all my chores done for the day and could waste my time on more frivolous pursuits. "I was planning to give it a try this afternoon."

His mouth pursed slightly, but to my relief, he didn't call me out on the delaying tactic. Maybe he'd realized I was doing all this with some reluctance, and so he thought it better not to push too hard. "It was on the news," he said cheerfully. "Did you see it?"

I hadn't; I generally didn't watch TV in the morning, finding it more relaxing to sit at the kitchen table with a cup of coffee and watch the birds cheerfully hopping around in the backyard. Every once in a while, I'd take my phone with me so I could do a quick scroll on Twitter or Instagram or whatever, but I definitely hadn't been in the mood for social media this particular morning, not when I guessed both feeds would probably be full of chatter about Tom Gallegos' murder.

"No," I replied. "Did they have anything new to offer?"

"Not really," Max said. He paused for a

moment so he could slide the Bronco into an open space across the street from Charlie's, the restaurant where we were headed, and then added, "Just the usual 'community in shock' and 'police are following all leads' kind of stuff. I suppose it's too soon for there to have been any real developments."

"And if there were, Chief DeVargas is probably keeping them pretty close to the vest," I said. "I doubt she wants to say or do anything that might tip off the murderer that she's on to him."

"Probably not," Max agreed, then turned off the engine. A small smile played around his mouth as he asked, "Ready?"

"Sure," I said, and put my fingers on the door handle so I could let myself out of the car.

Going out to eat with Max could definitely be...interesting. Sure, the locals were pretty much used to having him back in town by this point, and they definitely wouldn't do anything so gauche as to ask for an autograph or a selfie, but that didn't mean any random tourists in the vicinity might not do that very thing. We didn't get as many visitors as Santa Fe or even Albuquerque, but people often stopped in Las Vegas on their way to Denver, or swung by because they'd heard about the town's carefully preserved turn-of-the-century architecture and wanted to check it out for themselves.

And since Yelp thoughtfully provided tips to the entire world on the best places to eat in any given area, it wasn't as though there was anything like a "locals only" kind of establishment where the two of us could hide from the tourists.

Because I knew Max was used to the attention, I tried my best to act casual as we walked into the restaurant and went up to the hostess station. Standing there was a girl who looked as though she was probably still in high school, someone whose eyes widened as she took in her restaurant's latest visitor.

"Um...hi?" she said, the words ending on an upward inflection, as though she knew she shouldn't be asking a question but didn't know how else to contain her shock at seeing an honest-to-God movie star walking into the establishment where she worked. True, Max had been here at Charlie's several times since moving back to Las Vegas, but apparently they hadn't crossed paths before today.

"Hi," he said casually. "Got a table for two?"

"Um...yeah," the girl said, scrambling for a couple of menus. "Right this way."

She led us to a booth near the back, probably guessing that someone as high profile as Max Sullivan would prefer to be seated someplace where he wouldn't attract too much notice. Even so, I noted the way people glanced over at us, registered some surprise, and then studiously returned to their food so they wouldn't look as though they were gawking.

We sat down in the booth, its bright green vinyl-upholstered seats exactly the same as they'd been back in high school. In fact, the whole café didn't seem to have changed a bit even from when I was a little kid.

Of course, one huge difference between now and high school was that back then, I wouldn't have been sitting opposite Max Sullivan. He'd always been friendly—and did his best to make sure the bullies left me alone—but he also hadn't gone out on any breakfast dates with me.

Not that this was a date. No, it was only two friends getting together for a meal, with the added bonus of getting driven back downtown so I could retrieve my Subaru from one of the parking spaces behind Levitation Latte.

I knew I shouldn't be asking for anything more than that...even if deep down I couldn't keep myself from wishing for that very thing.

We both picked up our menus, mostly out of reflex, since the bill of fare also hadn't changed in more than ten years, and so we already knew pretty much everything on it. I decided to go for *machaca* —shredded roast beef and green chile sauce on top of scrambled eggs—while Max set down his menu and said, "Carne adovada and eggs, or huevos rancheros?"

"Well, have you had either one of those recently?" I inquired.

"I had huevos rancheros last week," he replied.

"Then there's your answer, right?"

He flashed me a smile, one he kept in place as our server approached—Maggie Milner, as much of a fixture at Charlie's as the green leatherette booths. She had to be in her late sixties at least, although her real age was a closely guarded secret, one she did her best to conceal with bleached platinum hair she always wore up in a twist and the same blue eyeshadow she'd probably had in her makeup bag since the 1970s.

Maybe there was the faintest flicker of surprise in her eyes as she saw me sitting there with Max, but she was too much of a professional to reveal anything more than that.

"What can I getcha?" she asked, pencil poised over her notepad. Even in high school, I'd been convinced the pad was a prop and that she really didn't need to write anything down, but I definitely was too chicken to come out and ask her point-blank.

"Coffee for me," Max said, and then sent me an inquiring glance.

"Hot tea, please," I said at once. They had good coffee at Charlie's, but it couldn't compete with mine. Besides, I'd already had a cup that morning, so I didn't need any more high-octane stuff than that to get me going.

"And to eat?"

Max and I placed our respective orders, and she headed off toward the kitchen after promising she'd be back with our drinks in a jif.

Once we were safely alone, he picked up the conversation right where we'd left off. "I am kind of bummed none of those news reports even mentioned that we were the ones who discovered Tom Gallegos' body."

Ah, Max. He always had to be in the limelight, even when the events in question only involved him tangentially. It was a trait I found endearing rather than annoying, because anyone could tell you that Max Sullivan didn't have a mean bone in his body. No, it was more that his was such an expansive personality and shone so brightly, it just seemed natural he should be the center of attention.

"Well," I said carefully, "I'm sure Chief DeVargas was just being cautious about what she said. After all, you were the center of a murder investigation only a month ago. She probably thought mentioning you would attract the wrong kind of attention."

"I was cleared of all charges," Max said at once, and I smiled.

"Yes, but you know how the media is."

When confronted with that obvious fact, he couldn't really argue with me. He settled against the back of the booth, looking thoughtful, just as Maggie returned with our coffee and tea.

"Breakfast'll be right up," she told us, and then hurried off again.

I hoped I'd have that kind of energy when I got to be her age.

For a moment, Max and I were both silent, since he needed to pause and put a tiny bit of cream and sugar in his coffee, and I needed to decide what I wanted from the little basket of tea Maggie had brought with my hot water. I settled on peppermint, mostly because I knew I'd have to read tea leaves later that day and didn't want to have anything remotely similar to the gunpowder green tea I often used for that kind of ritual.

Max's expression brightened after he took his first swallow of coffee. "I guess we'll just have to wait and see what other clues start popping up. In a town like this, rumors travel fast."

That they did. How exactly he intended to gather those rumors when he was isolated out at his ranch, I wasn't sure.

In the next moment, though, I learned exactly what he was expecting.

I should have known.

"People tell you all kinds of things, don't they?" he inquired, face a study in innocence.

Luckily, I knew him too well to fall for that kind of ploy. I picked up my cup of tea and said, "Max, I sell coffee and muffins. I'm not a shrink, or whatever."

"Well, yeah," he said, and swallowed some more of his coffee. "That doesn't mean people don't gossip when they're in your shop, right?"

"Sometimes," I allowed. "And sure, if I hear anything that sounds interesting, I'll pass it on to you. What I'm not going to do is start asking a bunch of leading questions. That's going to make people suspicious...and it could very well make the murderer a lot more cautious. We don't want anyone to think we're pursuing our own investigation or something."

Especially Chief DeVargas. I didn't think she could arrest me for being a snoop or anything like that, but I also didn't want to get on her bad side.

"That's true." Max glanced out the window beside our booth, but since it only overlooked the alley between the restaurant and the building next door, there wasn't a whole heck of a lot to see. "But I'm sure between your tea leaves and whatever you might overhear at the coffee shop, we'll definitely be on track to solve this before the police do."

Not for the first time, I wished I had his sunny optimism. He seemed to think that all we had to do was pick up a few decent clues, and we'd have the whole thing figured out and the key to the city handed over to us before you could say "New York minute."

I had my doubts as to whether everything would go that smoothly, but I decided it wasn't worth the argument. Maybe after I'd had a couple of completely inconclusive tea readings, Max would decide to join the rest of us mortals down here on earth.

"I guess we'll just have to see," I told him.

His brows drew together slightly, letting me know that wasn't exactly the response he'd been hoping for. However, Maggie came by with our food right then, and so I was saved from any further discussion for the moment.

After we'd both taken a few bites of our breakfasts, though, Max made it obvious he wasn't about to let the subject go. "You don't seem very enthusiastic about any of this."

"It's not that I'm not enthusiastic," I replied after I'd swallowed my mouthful of *machaca*. "It's just that I need to be careful I don't come off as too nosy. Like I said, I don't want to rouse anyone's suspicions."

That was a logical concern about the whole situation, so I didn't see how he could really argue the point much further. Apparently, he'd come to the same conclusion, because he only made a noncommittal sound and picked up one of the tortillas that had come with his meal so he could make a wrap out of some adovada and eggs.

And, to my relief, he seemed to have figured out I wasn't going to budge, since his next comments were about how he was putting together a big Thanksgiving dinner at the ranch and how he wanted to make sure I would come. This plan seemed a little far off in the future to me—Thanksgiving was still more than a month away—but I was only too glad to discuss something other than Tom Gallegos' murder. Ever since my grandmother Maureen had died, I'd spent Thanksgiving with Deanne and Mike. This year, though, I thought they'd understand why I wanted to beg off.

"I'll make pies," I said, my tone firm so Max would know the topic wasn't up for discussion.

He had the good grace to look sheepish. "Actually, I was kind of hoping you'd offer. Pumpkin and apple?"

"And chocolate cream, because I know that's your dad's favorite," I replied with a smile.

Max grinned back at me as he scooped some more adovada into his tortilla. "You're an angel."

"I wouldn't go so far as to say that," I said. "But I'm happy to make pies for Thanksgiving—and anything else you might need."

Of course, he rushed in to say that he would never expect one of his guests to prepare the whole meal, and said he planned to smoke a turkey and then order a bunch of sides from Kin, the restaurant at the Hotel Castañeda. Since I was acquainted with the chef at that particular place and knew he was amazing, I had to be satisfied with that. Maybe it wouldn't exactly be a home-cooked meal, but it should still be fabulous.

Now the only trick would be getting past the mystery of Tom Gallegos' murder so it wouldn't continue to dominate our lives.

CHAPTER 6

Shoveling It In

As promised, Max drove me over to Levitation Latte after breakfast so I could retrieve my car. It looked none the worse for wear after its night parked behind the building...not that I'd really expected it to. The poor thing sat outside at my place as well, and so it was its normal dusty self. Once a month, I took the Subaru to the car wash as my way of saying sorry for how I left it outside all the time instead of parking it in the garage, but I knew one of these days I really needed to roll up my sleeves and get the place cleaned out, if only to prove to myself I had the intestinal fortitude to go through the remainder of my grandmother's belongings and decide what stayed and what needed to be donated or tossed.

Max and I said our goodbyes, and I headed home, knowing I'd promised him I'd do a tea leaf reading today…and not really looking forward to the task.

What if I unearthed something he'd want to investigate right away?

I told myself the leaves weren't generally that clear-cut or reliable, but I wasn't sure whether I believed those inner reassurances. Just the month before, when Max asked me how accurate those readings were, I'd told him they were generally correct about seventy-five or eighty percent of the time…which meant my odds of getting a piece of information that wasn't completely useless weren't as high as I would have liked.

But I still made myself go through all the necessary steps of the ritual: choosing the correct tea—in this case, the gunpowder green tea whose leaves usually made lovely, easy-to-read patterns—heating the water and pouring it slowly over the leaves, and holding in my mind the question I wanted answered, which was simple enough.

Who killed Tom Gallegos?

I poured myself a cup and sat for a moment or two as I waited for it to cool, my gaze fixed on the garden scene outside my window. The only flowers hanging on by this point were several clumps of late-blooming asters I'd planted specifically so I'd have some fall color in my garden, but the trees themselves were now displays of blazing gold, warm and somehow comforting. I loved this time of year,

even though fall presaged winter's snows and the
dark, short days that still didn't seem to pass
quickly enough.

A hand laid against the side of my cup told
me it was now cool enough to drink, so I picked it
up, still doing my best to remain calm and
focused, and then took a sip, followed by another.
No huge swallows, no rushing. This was all about
quiet and reflection, about letting the energy of
the tea enter me and allow me to interpret what it
had to say.

At last the teacup was empty, and I turned it
upside down over its saucer to allow the last few
drops to drip onto the flat surface. Now the cup
was ready to provide whatever information it
wanted to impart.

That first look seemed to offer a bunch of
nondescript blobs and nothing else. A little tremor
of worry went through me when I thought I saw a
heart, and I wondered if Tom Gallegos' murder
really was going to turn out to be an affair of
passion, just as Max had first postulated.

But no, I realized as I squinted at the interior of
the cup, that wasn't a heart. It actually looked more
like a three-leaf clover to me.

I stared down into the cup, a frown pulling at
my mouth. In general, a clover—even a three-leaf
one—was a symbol of good luck.

Somehow, I found it hard to believe there'd

been any good luck involved in Tom Gallegos' murder.

Okay, I'd file that one away for later. Maybe after I scrutinized the rest of the leaves and found more symbols to interpret, the clover would make more sense.

But I didn't see anything else of much significance, except a small blob near the bottom of the cup with a slender line of leaves leading off to the right that vaguely resembled a shovel or a spade. Since a spade was also usually a sign of good luck— at least, that's what all my books on tasseography said—seeing it now didn't seem to make any more sense than the three-leaf clover had.

With a sigh, I rose from my chair, picked up the cup and saucer, and then washed them off and dried them with a tea towel I had hanging from a magnetic hook on the side of the refrigerator. The fine porcelain was too fragile to go in the dishwasher, so I always made sure to clean it by hand.

After I was done with that task, I went back over to the kitchen window and stared out into the yard for a long moment. The day was sunny and bright, not as warm as it looked—I'd had to pull a sweater on over my top before heading out to breakfast that morning—but gorgeous nonetheless.

Maybe I should go outside and get some fresh

air, see if that might provide some clarity regarding the symbols I'd seen inside the cup.

Unfortunately, a solid half-hour spent cleaning up the last straggling veggies in my plot in the community garden down the street didn't appear to offer any real illumination. No matter how I tried to look at it, I couldn't understand how getting throttled and then dumped in a corn maze could possibly be construed as good luck.

Well, these sorts of inaccurate readings happened from time to time. It was entirely possible that my reluctance to meddle in the murder investigation had spilled over into the arrangement of the leaves despite my best attempts at maintaining focus.

Either way, I'd told Max I would call him when I had some information to pass on, so I figured I might as well get it over with. He'd be disappointed, but there wasn't much I could do about that.

However, I poured myself some iced tea first, then took the glass and my phone with me into the living room, where I could at least be comfortable on the couch when I made the call.

His phone rang several times, and I found myself hoping I'd get his voicemail. Somehow, it seemed easier to deliver bad news that way.

No such luck, though—he picked up on the third ring.

"Hey, Skye," he said, tone way too excited for my taste. "What'd you find?"

"Nothing much," I replied. "The only clear symbols I saw in the cup are both related to good luck, and I don't see how that can possibly apply here."

Since this was Max I was talking to, he sounded undaunted as he said, "Well, maybe there's something else we're not seeing here. Maybe the mayor had gambling debts or something, and that's why he was murdered."

"I've never heard a single thing about Tom Gallegos having a gambling problem," I said dubiously. "That's the kind of thing that's hard to keep secret in a town as small as this, especially when you're talking about a person who's sort of a public figure. Anyway, if he really did gamble and was lucky at it, he wouldn't have debts, right?"

A pause. "Okay, maybe," Max allowed, now sounding a little less chipper than he had a moment earlier. "But maybe he had a big win, and someone found out and killed him to get the money."

I had to give Max credit—apparently, his capacity to come up with shady scenarios was boundless. If the acting thing ever fell through, he could always switch over to writing screenplays or something.

Since I hated to keep throwing cold water on his ideas...even while I knew I needed to be the voice of reason here...I kept my tone gentle as I said, "I suppose I could see that happening, but if he really had won big at one of the casinos, wouldn't it have made more sense to mug him as he was leaving the place instead of trying to pull off a murder at an event as public as the harvest festival?"

Another long pause. "I hate it when you're right."

Now I was the one grinning. "We don't know if I'm right. Right now, we don't know much of anything."

"You'll try again, won't you?"

"Maybe later," I said, even though the thought of having to do the ritual again while asking the same apparently useless question didn't appeal to me very much. "But I need to give it a little space. It's never a good idea to do a reading on the same question twice in the same day."

Which was pretty much a rule I'd made up on the spot, although it seemed a good one to follow. If the leaves didn't want to talk, there was no use in being pushy. We needed to cultivate some patience...something Max had never been particularly good at.

To my relief, he didn't nag me to keep going. Quite possibly, he'd realized that this was my area of expertise, and so he needed to defer to my guidance. At least, I hoped that's what he was thinking.

"Well," he said, "you'll be back at the shop tomorrow, so maybe you'll pick up some intel there."

I wasn't nearly as sure about that. On the other hand, Kyle Isaacs, my erstwhile deputy boyfriend, often let slip things about an investigation that he really shouldn't be discussing with a civilian. I could only hope he'd be as loose-lipped about this particular case as he'd been about the murder of Perry Lockhart.

"We'll see," I said lightly.

Max seemed to take the hint, because he only said, "Thanks for the call, Skye. Let me know if anything else comes up."

"I will. Have a good rest of your day."

We ended the call there, and I set the phone down on the coffee table before reaching for my iced tea. Current mood? Mixture of relief...and disappointment. While I really hadn't wanted to talk about Tom Gallegos' murder investigation anymore, somewhere deep inside, I'd still been hoping that Max might have asked me over to his place for dinner.

But no such invitation had been forthcoming, probably because he figured we'd already had breakfast and settled our business, and so there was no reason for us to spend any additional time together today.

No reason except wanting to be with me as much as possible, that is.

Clearly, his thoughts didn't run along those same paths. No, I was his friend and his sounding board, and that was about it. I supposed I should be grateful that he didn't show any interest in having any kind of a personal life while he was staying here in Las Vegas. The pickings were kind of slim on the ground, but he could have found someone if he really wanted to.

Even, as much as my stomach roiled at the thought, Raylene Bryant. She'd been looking pretty damn good at the harvest festival last night.

Don't be an idiot, I scolded myself as I took another sip of iced tea. *I think Max would rather be celibate for the rest of his life than take up with Raylene again. He learned his lesson on that one.*

I wanted to hope so. Unfortunately, only time would tell.

My sleep that night was more restless than usual, although not because of any prophetic dreams, thank God. I dreamed about tornadoes, a recurring nightmare I seemed to have whenever too much was weighing on my mind, even if the particulars of those dreams might change.

Because of my restless evening, I knew I was

crankier than usual when I rolled into Levitation Latte about fifteen minutes late. Not that anyone was around to notice my tardiness, since Deanne always came in a half hour after I did, generally around six o'clock.

Still, I was annoyed with myself, knowing I'd have to hustle to make sure all the baked goods were ready and cooled down enough to be placed in the bakery case by the time we opened at seven. And although I'd already had a hurried cup of coffee at home before coming in to work, I still poured myself a cup from the first batch I brewed, knowing I needed the extra fuel to overcome the effects of my crappy night's sleep.

My irritation must not have died down very much, because almost as soon as Deanne came into the kitchen where I was pulling the first batch of pumpkin chocolate chunk muffins out of the oven, she took one look at me and said, "What's wrong? Didn't your breakfast with Max go okay?"

"It went fine," I told her. "But he wants to go full Nancy Drew on this thing, and I don't know whether that's such a great idea. Also, I tried to do a reading about Tom Gallegos' murder yesterday and got a big fat nothing."

She squeezed her oversized purse into one of the little cubbies we kept in one corner for our personal belongings, then reached for the nearby hook where her apron hung. After she'd finished tying it around her waist, she said, "Well, that's not good."

"No, it isn't," I replied. "Or maybe it is good—maybe it's a sign that I should be keeping my nose out of the whole thing." I paused there. My friend's expression was one of concern and didn't show any sign that she had something important to tell me, but I figured I'd ask anyway. "I don't suppose you heard anything at church yesterday."

At once, she shook her head. As usual, she had her long blonde hair pulled back in a ponytail, and wore just enough makeup that she looked fresh-faced and cheerful, rather than crabby about being awake and alert at such an ungodly hour.

"No," she said at once. "I mean, everyone was talking about the way you and Max found the mayor's body, and a whole lot of theories were flying about what really happened, but I didn't hear anything that sounded like it was some new proof that had surfaced or anything like that."

About what I'd expected, but I couldn't prevent a stab of disappointment from going through me. At the back of my mind, I'd been hoping that Chief DeVargas had been working on the case all day and had already found some solid leads.

No such luck, obviously.

Deanne peered at my face. "What did you see in the tea leaves?"

I went over to the long table we used for food prep and started mixing up a batch of cranberry muffins, something I could do in my sleep since they were a flavor I offered year-round.

"Nothing," I said. "Or at least, nothing that seemed as if it had any bearing on the case. A couple of good-luck symbols."

Her nose wrinkled. "That doesn't make any sense."

"Exactly."

Still looking confused, she headed out into the coffee shop proper, where I had the first batch of Italian roast already brewed and ready to go. A minute later, she was back in the kitchen, a mug cradled in her hands. She took a sip, then said, "Well, it'll come to you."

"Or it won't," I replied over the whir of the mixer. By that point, we were used to pitching our voices loud enough to get past the sound of my trusty KitchenAid doing its magic on the latest batch of muffins, so I didn't bother to wait until I was done before adding, "I told Max that maybe nothing would come to me at all, since it's not like I have much of a personal connection to the case."

Deanne seemed to consider those words as she took a couple more swallows of Italian roast. "That makes sense. Still, you never know. I mean, you don't always have much of a personal interest in the results of your readings for clients, either."

That was true. Of course I wanted the readings to be positive ones, and not something that might dig up clues to a spouse's infidelity or something similarly earth-shattering, but it also was true that my clients weren't my besties the way Deanne or Max were. They were neighbors or acquaintances, friends of the family, that kind of thing.

And yet I never seemed to have too much trouble getting people the answers they needed, which meant a personal connection wasn't the be-all, end-all when it came to reading tea leaves.

"Maybe it's the universe telling me to butt out," I said, and she grinned.

"Maybe. Anyway, I'm going to go out and get the tables wiped down, and make sure all the lids and straws are stocked."

I gave her a thumbs-up, and she went out into the shop to perform the early morning ritual of tidying up and doing whatever was necessary to get the place ready for that day's opening, now only about forty minutes away. It would be close with this batch of muffins, but I thought I could make it work.

Which I did, sliding the luscious cranberry confections into the bakery case just as Deanne headed over to unlock the front door. I allowed myself an inner sigh of relief, glad that my late arrival to work hadn't slowed down the morning routine too much.

As usual, we had the normal early rush of people picking up coffee and pastries on their way to work. Unfortunately, no one seemed too inclined to be chatty, or at least, not chatty about the mayor's untimely demise. Only Lucy Margolis, my neighbor across the street, took a moment to send me a solicitous glance as I popped the lid on her caramel macchiato.

"And you're doing all right, Skye?" she asked. "I mean, after what happened at the harvest festival."

"I'm fine," I replied, and it wasn't even a lie. Yes, I felt awful about what had happened to poor Tom Gallegos, and equally horrible about what his family must be going through, but it wasn't a tragedy that had touched me personally. And since she'd asked, I ventured, "You haven't heard anything more about who might be responsible, have you?"

As I'd thought, she shook her head at once. "No, there was nothing in the paper this morning, only that Mayor Gallegos' death was still under investigation." A pause, and then she went on, her voice lowering a bit, "Although I did notice something odd at the festival."

My ears pricked up immediately. "'Odd'?" I repeated, hoping I didn't sound too eager.

Lucy made a dismissive gesture with one hand, even as she said, "Oh, it was probably nothing. It's just that I noticed Raylene Bryant going up to the mayor right after his speech and talking to him, seeming a little too earnest. She had a hand on his arm, but I couldn't hear what they were saying."

Yes, that was strange. I didn't think Raylene even knew Tom Gallegos.

Unless....

Lucy said aloud the horrible suspicion that had just crossed my mind. "You don't think they were having an affair, do you?"

"Oh, I doubt it," I said, although my mind raced with possibilities. Everything I'd heard about Tom made it seem as though he was a devoted family man...but what if he wasn't? And Raylene always had been the type to glom on to the nearest alpha male. Maybe hooking up with the mayor was just the next step.

Lucy's lips pursed. "I didn't want to think it, either," she replied. "But Raylene's gone through a lot lately and maybe was feeling lonely."

About all I could do was shrug. While defending Raylene Bryant definitely hadn't been on my agenda that day, I found myself saying, "I'm sure it was perfectly innocent."

"You're probably right," Lucy said. "I suppose I'm just trying to find motives where there really aren't any."

You and me both, I thought, and said, "I hope the police can figure it out soon. I hate to think the murderer is still out there somewhere."

Lucy shivered a little. "You and me both. It's awful to have had two deaths like this almost back to back. That's unheard of for us." She took her macchiato from me and said, "I've got to be going. You be careful, Skye."

"I will," I said automatically, although I didn't think I had much to be worried about. It wasn't as if I was alone in the coffee shop and besides, I didn't see any reason why anyone would want to target me. The tea leaves hadn't told me much, but I still had a feeling in my bones that Tom's had been a personal death, that there had been a motive behind his murder which had nothing to do with simple robbery.

Anyway, if anyone really had grand larceny on their mind, Levitation Latte wasn't exactly a prime target. There were stores on Bridge Street with expensive art and Native American jewelry in their inventories, not to mention much more money in their cash registers. My Breville espresso machine had cost me a pretty penny, but I didn't think it was the sort of thing that would exactly be easy to fence.

And while I would have been all too happy to believe Raylene Evans was involved in Tom's death, again, she just wasn't big and strong enough to haul two hundred pounds of dead weight anywhere, let alone pull it over the high walls of the corn maze. Plus, throttling someone with a rope just didn't seem to be her style.

Poison, sure.

A little after nine, Kyle Isaacs came in to the shop. He wore his uniform and appeared a very different man from the guy in the cowboy-punk getup he'd had on for his canceled gig at the festival.

I perked up immediately. Kyle didn't usually have that kind of an effect on me, but I had to hope maybe he was in possession of some information about the Gallegos case that hadn't yet made it to the local newspaper.

"Hey, Kyle," I said, doing my best to sound casual. "Coffee, or maybe a latte?"

"Coffee and one of those pumpkin chocolate chunk muffins," he replied as he came closer to the counter, then handed over the go-cup that sometimes seemed as much a part of his uniform as his badge. On the other side of the room, Deanne appeared to be occupied wiping down a table, but I could tell her ears had pricked up as soon as my deputy ex appeared on the scene.

"Coming right up," I told him. I got to work pouring a venti Italian roast into his cup, then bent down so I could retrieve one of the requested muffins from the bakery case. As I handed them over, I said, still trying to play it cool, "How's it going?"

Obviously, my casual act hadn't fooled him for a second, because he said, "There isn't much new to report, if that's what you're asking."

I put my hands on my hips and sent him a wounded look. "I wasn't."

"Sure." He smiled then, hazel eyes clearly amused. No, he wasn't as good-looking as Max—who could be?—but Kyle was definitely attractive enough, even if he'd never been able to exactly get my motor running. A brief glance around the shop—the morning rush had passed, so he was currently our only customer—must have told him it was safe to go on, though, as he added, "I mean, we know Mayor Gallegos must have been killed right after he gave his speech at the opening of the festival, because he'd already been dead for a couple of hours before you found him."

Which I'd already guessed, but it was good to know my hunch had been verified. I remained silent, though, realizing that the best way to hear more was to let Kyle go on with his story and not ask too many questions. That way, he could justify our conversation to himself as harmless gossip, rather than responding to a friend's interrogation.

"But we don't know much more than that," he went on as he broke off a piece of his pumpkin chocolate chunk muffin and helped himself to a bite. "I mean, right now the chief thinks he must have been killed somewhere else and dumped in the maze, just because there were way too many people coming and going around there for his body to have lain unnoticed for hours, but we haven't been able to find any evidence to prove her theory."

Again, pretty much the same thing I'd been thinking. Would the detectives even be able to find evidence of the perpetrator coming at the maze from the outside and tipping the body over the bales of hay that made up its walls? Plaza Park had grass everywhere—a little yellowed from frost at this point, but still—and so it wasn't the sort of thing that would easily preserve footprints for analysis. Also, with so many people wandering around the place during the festival, the killer's tracks must have been overlaid by those of a whole lot of innocent bystanders.

"Well, I'm sure she'll figure it out," I said, figuring that sort of reassuring statement would be harmless enough.

Kyle blew out a breath and ate another bite of muffin, washing it down with some Italian roast. His expression wasn't exactly morose—it was hard to look too sad while eating that kind of midmorning snack—but I could tell he wasn't happy with the current state of affairs. It would have been so much easier for everyone involved if the killer had been sloppy and left a definite trail for the police chief and her detectives to find.

"Maybe," he allowed. "At first, I thought it was

crazy that someone would even think about committing a crime like that—you know, in such a public place with so many people milling around—but now I kind of get it. Any evidence that might have been left behind would get completely destroyed by all the people who passed through that maze." He stopped there, sending me a grimly humorous glance. "You know how many?"

I shook my head. Estimating the size of crowds had never been my forte, but I had to believe at least a thousand people had come and gone from the festival before it was cut abruptly short by Max's and my grim discovery. Most likely, not all of them had explored the corn maze—you do that sort of thing once, and that's probably enough to last you for a while—and yet it definitely must have been enough to make the crime scene an utter mess.

"Four hundred and twenty-three," he said, looking proud of himself for remembering the exact number. "At least, that's the number of tickets that Lisbeth—the girl who was working the corn maze—had collected. Obviously, we cordoned off the crime scene and did our best, but trying to figure out what was left behind by the killer and what had been dropped by the people walking through the maze before he dumped the mayor's body there is going to be pretty much impossible."

"I can see that," I responded before deciding I

might as well ask. It wasn't as though I'd been peppering Kyle with questions the whole time we were talking. "What kind of things did you find?"

His shoulders lifted, and he broke off another piece of muffin. "The usual. Gum wrappers...pieces of popcorn...strands of hair. Some discarded cups and taco wrappers." He made a face, as though wondering which of his neighbors had been big enough slobs to just drop their garbage in the corn maze rather than dispose of it in one of the trash cans that were placed strategically around the park. "But I kind of doubt the killer would be dumb enough to leave anything like that behind."

No, probably not. Whoever had killed Tom Gallegos, they were clearly cagey enough to haul a dead body into the corn maze and dump it there without anyone being the wiser. They certainly wouldn't have dropped a taco wrapper covered in their DNA anywhere nearby.

The strands of hair, though...maybe that was the lead the police needed to track down their murderer.

"Are you analyzing the hair you found?" I inquired, knowing that was probably too pointed a question even as I asked it.

To my relief, Kyle didn't tell me to mind my own business, or that he couldn't divulge anything about that particular aspect of the case. "Yeah, we sent it all off to the lab," he said. "But the only real way that would help would be if we could cross-reference all the matches with the people who'd bought tickets to the corn maze. If there was an oddball strand, then that might point to our killer."

"Well, why can't you do that?" I asked, even as I guessed I was missing the point.

Luckily, he was too nice to call attention to my obvious stupidity. "Cash only for the tickets," he said. "No way to track that. So, even though the hair might have helped us, because there wasn't any record of who went into the corn maze, we're kind of stuck."

"I'm sorry," I said at once. "That has to be frustrating."

He picked up his coffee and took a philosophical sip. "More for the chief and the detectives on the case. Luckily, I'm just a lowly deputy, so no one expects me to solve any crimes."

"You're not lowly." Then, because he looked a little too cheered up by my comment, maybe thinking I'd offered him an opening to try asking me out again, I hurriedly added, "It's a bummer you didn't get to play, though."

"No biggie," Kyle said. Now seeming even cheerier than the moment before, he went on, "Actually, we're playing at Blackie's tomorrow night. You should come on down."

I allowed myself an inner groan, even as I did

my best to keep my expression neutral. Blackie's was kind of a dive bar down on CanAm Highway, but it was one of the few places in Las Vegas that had live music on a regular basis. Clearly, Kyle thought it would be just great if I showed up and played groupie.

But then I realized I had the perfect way to dodge his off-hand invitation. "Sounds like fun," I told him, doing my best to keep my tone casual. "But Tuesday's a school night. I'm up before the crack of dawn, remember?"

At once, his face fell. "Oh, right. Forgot about that. I've got Wednesday and Thursday off this week, so it worked fine for me. I'll have to ask Dawn to see if she can schedule the band for a Friday or Saturday sometime so you can come see us play."

Dawn Rogers ran Blackie's. She was exactly the kind of tough-looking woman you'd expect to see managing a place like that, somewhere in her late forties or early fifties, with impressively tatted arms, multiple piercings, and hair that never seemed to be the same color from one week to the next. I had no doubt that if anyone tried to tell her the way she looked wasn't appropriate for a woman her age, she would have kicked them right through a wall.

"That sounds good," I said, figuring I should be able to come up with some sort of excuse for bowing out if Kyle and his band ever did manage to get a weekend gig at the bar. It wasn't that I wanted to crush his tender feelings, but I also didn't want to give him false hope.

The radio on his shoulder came to life then, calling out a string of numbers and an address, and he picked it up and said, "On my way." A glance at me, and he added, "Sorry. Gotta go."

"No worries," I replied. "Duty calls. I get it."

He hurriedly downed the remainder of his coffee and hastened out of the shop. After he was gone, Deanne...who'd been pretending to tidy up during the entire conversation...shot me an inquiring glance.

"Get anything good?" she asked.

"Not really," I said. "A few bits and pieces. They're definitely not anywhere close to figuring out who killed Tom Gallegos."

As I spoke, a sinking feeling came over me.

Like it or not, it sure looked as though Max and I might have to be the ones to solve this case.

CHAPTER 7

Speaking in Tongues

To my relief, the remainder of that day was pretty uneventful, and we were able to close right on time. Deanne and I headed to our respective homes, although I thought she would probably end up having a much more peaceful evening than I.

Well, I could thank Max for that. The whole drive home—all five minutes of it—I kept thinking about what he'd said to me at the harvest festival about not developing my talent, about how I was like that kid who could play Mozart by ear but who stubbornly refused to take piano lessons.

Maybe it was time to see if I could make these so-called talents of mine a little stronger, a little more reliable. Exactly how I was supposed to do something like that, I really didn't know, but after I'd put together a caprese salad for dinner and poured myself a glass of primitivo, I figured I'd do the same thing millions of other people did when they were trying to learn about a subject and didn't know where they should start.

I went to YouTube.

There were literally thousands of psychics and astrologers and self-proclaimed witches on the streaming platform, and I honestly had no real idea where I should even start. However, I wasn't trying to dissect my birth chart, and I wasn't trying to cast prosperity spells...although some of the videos on love spells were just a little too tempting.

Was it possible I could lure Max Sullivan to my side simply by sleeping with a chunk of rose quartz under my pillow, or by creating a spell jar filled with a specific set of herbs and crystals and lighting a candle next to it for a week?

Even if those methods might work...and I honestly wasn't sure whether they would...doing something like that felt like cheating. I'd rather go my whole life with Max as only a friend and nothing more than resort to those sorts of tactics to make him fall in love with me. If he couldn't be with me on honest terms, then better not at all.

After about forty minutes of surfing around, I finally landed on someone who sounded as though she might be able to help me. True, she called herself "Madame Wanda," and she wore so many scarves and amulets that it was hard to tell where they left off and her plump figure began, but at least she seemed focused on developing a person's inner powers rather than casting love spells or telling me why my Jupiter in Sagittarius should make me more fearless than I actually was.

Also, some of those YouTube witches were a little intimidating. They had perfectly made-up faces and expertly styled hair, and looked as though they'd just gotten dressed for their latest batch of Instagram selfies rather than offering any sort of practical magic advice.

Practical magic. Right. There was absolutely nothing practical about what I was attempting to do.

But I reassured myself that I did have some small kind of talent. Otherwise, my tea leaf readings wouldn't be so accurate, and I wouldn't have dreams that often came true. Maybe it was a huge leap from those quiet sorts of magic to actually casting spells or whatever, but I knew I needed to try. It was entirely possible that I'd never be anything more than someone who ran a coffee shop in an out-of-the-way town in northern New Mexico, and yet...

...and yet, I knew I'd kick myself from now to the end of time if I didn't see whether I was capable of doing anything more than that.

"Find a way to center yourself," Madame Wanda intoned, and I paused the video so I could gulp down the remnants of my primitivo and then take my empty glass and plate into the kitchen. After stowing them in the dishwasher, I returned to the dining room table, where my laptop waited for me. I'd paused at an unfortunate moment, with Madame Wanda's fuchsia-lipsticked mouth open in a wide "O," so I hurriedly unpaused the video so I wouldn't start giggling and lose what little bit of concentration I'd managed to scrape together.

Since Madame Wanda herself was sitting on a chair as overstuffed as she was, I guessed it was okay for me to be seated on a dining room chair rather than on the floor in a lotus position or whatever. I sat upright, hands resting on my knees, and drew in a breath.

"Focus is everything," she went on. "Reach inside yourself to find the spark of your magic. It lives deep within, but will come forth when called. Imagine it like a warm glow surrounding you, infusing every cell in your body. This is the vital force, your *chi*, your *mana*. Let it come forth and do your bidding."

The urge to giggle was almost irresistible—did she really think people would buy this stuff?—but I told myself I needed to focus, to be as serious as possible. Otherwise, I should have blown off Max's comments, gone into the living room, and put my feet up on the couch so I could watch TV before going to bed at my usual weekday nine o'clock.

Okay. Golden glow. Magic spark. *Chi...mana.*

Whatever either of those things was.

Strangely, though, I thought I felt something stirring deep inside. An odd warmth began to flood through my midsection, flowing out to my fingertips, just as Madame Wanda had described.

What the heck? Was this stuff...real?

I blinked and opened my eyes. The video was paused again, even though I knew I hadn't reached over to touch my laptop's keys.

But that wasn't the strangest thing.

No, that would be the weird sparkly stuff flowing out of my fingertips and wrapping itself around me in a glowing cocoon.

I gasped and stood up so quickly that the chair fell over and hit the floor with a *bang*. At once, the shimmering gold tendrils that had emerged from my fingers disappeared as if they had never been there at all.

Maybe I shouldn't have had that glass of wine.

No, I wasn't drunk, or anything close to it. Whatever I'd just seen, it had been real.

Which meant that maybe I could summon it again.

I closed my eyes and breathed in and out, concentrating on the core of my being, visualizing that odd golden glow. A warmth that wrapped itself around my hands and arms told me it was happening again.

Cautiously, I cracked an eyelid. Yes, there it was, all shimmering and filled with dancing light, like animated glitter. This stuff, however, wouldn't leave an unholy mess everywhere like the real thing.

Because this wasn't glitter.

It was magic.

An odd little shiver...not exactly fear, not exactly excitement, but an unsettling mixture of both...ran through my body, and I made myself pull in a breath, hoping that might help to steady me. Whether it really worked or not, I didn't know, but I figured it was a place to start.

Not sure exactly what I should do next, I focused on the bowl full of autumn gourds at the center of the table. Then I extended one hand and made a gentle upward movement toward the ceiling.

At once, the gourds floated up and out of the bowl, and began to circle around one another in a complicated sort of dance. How they knew to do that, I had no idea, because it wasn't as if I'd directed them to make those particular movements. No, it was more as if the magic had taken hold of an image that had flitted through my brain, one that visualized the gourds making those intricate patterns, and had just run with it.

It seemed clear enough to me that if magic could be this powerful, then I'd have to be pretty darn careful about what I directed it to do.

As soon as that particular thought went through my head, it was as if I'd thrown a bucket of cold water over the whole setup. All the gourds fell to the table in a series of thumps and bumps, some of them rolling onto the floor. Luckily, they missed the bowl and didn't seem to do any damage to the tabletop.

The only casualty was one bumpy squash, which appeared to have hit the edge of the tabletop and then split in half. Once I'd recovered myself, I hurried to pick up the bits and pieces, and then went into the kitchen to get some paper towels to clean up the rest of the soupy gourd guts that had gotten splattered on the shining wood surface.

Another pause to gather up the rest of the spilled gourds and return them to their bowl, and then I stood there for a moment, staring at the squash that had been dancing above the table only a few minutes earlier. As I set down the roll of paper towels, I realized my hands were shaking.

I'd done it. I'd used magic—*real* magic, not just swirling leaves around in a teacup and hoping for the best.

All right, that was a form of magic as well, if not exactly as spectacular as the feat I'd just performed. And damn it, I wished I'd had the foresight to get out my phone and film the entire episode. Otherwise, I didn't see how I'd ever get anyone to believe I'd just made a bunch of gourds rise up out of a bowl and fly around in midair before they went splat.

Then again...did I *want* anyone to know about this?

Deanne and I confided in each other about almost everything. Certainly, she was the only person in Las Vegas who knew my deep, dark secret about being crazy in love with Max Sullivan. But this was a whole other ball of wax.

This was magic.

I stood there for a moment, staring at the gourds where they rested in the bowl, looking completely innocent and not as though they'd just performed an aerial ballet a minute earlier.

Should I try again?

Or maybe attempt something different?

Or maybe I should realize I'd performed enough miracles for the day and call it a night.

Unsure, I bent down to my laptop and unpaused Madame Wanda's video, figuring I might as well watch it through to the end and see whether she had any pearls of wisdom to impart when it came to performing multiple feats of magic in a short period of time.

Unfortunately, the rest of the video only consisted of more directions on how to concentrate and focus to awaken your magic...and if this short introduction to developing your powers wasn't sufficient, well, then, all you had to do was visit her website and use code "magicalme" to get twenty percent off her complete course, now available for the low price of just $199.

I blew out a breath and shut my laptop. It seemed as though I was on my own now...unless I wanted to fork over two hundred bucks to get additional instruction. Maybe it would be worth it...or maybe Madame Wanda already taught me everything I needed to know.

On the surface, that assertion sounded pretty arrogant. So, I'd managed to accomplish a showy parlor trick. That didn't mean my apparently expanding magic could help much with figuring out who actually killed Tom Gallegos.

But despite those inner admonitions, I couldn't help feeling tingly all over, shocked that these weird gifts I'd carried within me for most of my life had been able to manage something so beyond belief. How was this even possible? I read tea leaves and sometimes had "true" dreams, which seemed a far cry from getting a bunch of gourds to fly through the air.

On the other hand....

Max's analogy about music came to mind just then. Maybe I was more like someone who'd spent her whole life playing cello and then decided to take up the guitar. The two instruments were very different, but the fundamentals of being able to read music were the same in both cases. All I'd done was put aside my cello and instead strapped on an electric guitar.

Somehow, thinking about the situation that way made me feel a little less uneasy about what had just happened. I had a lot more work to do to figure out exactly what I could and couldn't manage with these strange gifts of mine, but something inside was telling me I needed to call it a night. It was a little early to go to bed, but I could go upstairs and draw a bath, pick up a book, and let myself relax, something I rarely had much time for these days.

Maybe in the morning I'd have a better idea of exactly what I should do next.

An extra cup of French roast when I got to the shop the next day didn't help much in terms of providing me with the mental clarity I so desperately needed. I still hadn't decided whether I should tell Deanne about what had happened the night before, or whether I should try practicing some more parlor tricks before I revealed that my supposed magical talents had just made a huge kind of quantum leap.

After swallowing the remnants of my coffee, I headed back to the storeroom to get a fresh batch of paper napkins for the dispenser on the counter, since it was just about out. I'd put in two batches of muffins already, and the mingled aromas of pumpkin spice and blueberry filled the air in the kitchen as I passed through, not discordant at all, but somehow managing to play nicely with each other and be both sweet and sharp at the same time.

Just as I was getting the napkins down from a shelf, Tilly, the stray cat that I and several of the other merchants on the street had adopted, came in through the little door I'd installed for her and began nosing around the bowls of water and cat food I'd refilled as soon as I got in this morning. Even though I knew Tilly had various feeding spots up and down Bridge Street, I liked to flatter myself that she came by Levitation Latte more than any of the other shops and restaurants, probably because I made sure to always order top-of-the-line food and treats for her.

She was a big black cat, with short, thick fur and striking green eyes. Almost at once, she started eating the Science Diet salmon dry food I'd put out for her, showing that whatever she'd been up to all evening, it hadn't been chasing mice and consuming them as late night snacks.

I watched her for a moment, glad she was hungry...and glad I could be here for her. Not for the first time, I wondered how far she roamed, whether she stuck around Las Vegas's downtown or ranged farther afield as the mood struck her. Either way, she was a very independent cat, and showed absolutely no interest in settling down and being my house pet...or anyone else's.

In the next moment, though, a sudden thought struck me. A cat like Tilly, who wandered far and wide, might be in the perfect position to see all sorts of things that people wouldn't want noticed. I mean, who paid any particular attention to a stray cat?

For all I knew, she'd witnessed Tom Gallegos' murder and knew exactly who the killer was.

That might have been true, but since cats couldn't talk, she wouldn't exactly be the most helpful witness.

Unless....

As soon as the thought entered my mind, I wanted to push it away. The idea was absolutely crazy. It was one thing to make those gourds at my house do their happy dance and fall to the table afterward, but getting a cat to talk?

I glanced down at my watch. Five forty-four. Deanne would be here in about fifteen minutes, give or take. I could try casting a spell to see if Tilly could talk, and then reverse it before my best friend showed up for work. She'd never have to know... and maybe the cat could provide some much-needed information.

Well, except for the part where I had absolutely no idea how to even begin crafting that kind of spell. I was no expert, but the bits and pieces I'd seen while I was surfing around on YouTube had told me that casting spells was a complicated process involving candles and oils and feathers and God knows what else. I certainly didn't have any of those items on hand; this was a coffee shop, not a witch's apothecary.

Then again....

The night before, I hadn't done anything particularly special when I made those gourds go flying above the dining room table. I'd merely set an intention in my mind, a sort of visualization, and then had sent the magic I'd seen flowing from my fingertips spiraling upward to catch the gourds in its golden net. Maybe I only needed to do something similar now.

I closed my eyes and thought of Madame Wanda's words from her video, about how I was supposed to focus on the magic in the core of my being, the strange gift that seemed to be entwined with my DNA the same way as the color of my eyes or the shape of my mouth.

And there it was, that warmth in the pit of my stomach...and the same shimmery gold flowing from my fingertips as I opened my eyes. Through all this, Tilly kept munching away at her Science Diet, completely oblivious to the woman standing a few feet away with strands of glitter emanating from her hands.

Now or never.

Fixing my gaze on the big black cat, I said, "Tilly, I give you the power of speech. Now you will be able to talk just like a human being."

As I spoke, the glittery magic dust or whatever it was floated from my fingers and wrapped itself around the cat as she finished the last few bites of kitty kibble in her bowl. One of her ears twitched a little, but that was the only response I got to my impromptu spell.

So much for thinking that my hocus had any pocus in it.

I set my hands on my hips, wondering if I should give it another try. Unfortunately, the timer on the oven went off then, and I had to hurry into the kitchen to pull the trays of muffins out before they got a little too browned for my taste. Usually, I'd have another batch ready to pop into the oven, but since I'd been preoccupied with the cat, I'd sort of fallen down on the job there.

Well, at this point, another small delay wouldn't make much of a difference.

Moving just as quickly, I returned to the storeroom. Tilly was now done with her food and had begun grooming herself, presumably to make sure no pesky kibble crumbs had marred her smooth black fur.

Even though it seemed as if my spell had been a dismal failure, I couldn't help venturing, "Tilly? Are you sure you don't want to say anything?"

She stopped licking her paw and set it down on the floor. Cool green eyes met mine. "And exactly what were you expecting me to say?"

I took a shocked step backward and bumped into the mixing table, which prevented me from retreating any further.

Okay, I'd cast the spell, but I hadn't expected it to work. Not really.

"Um," I hedged, then quickly added, "How was your breakfast?"

"Fine, I suppose." Her green eyes narrowed. "Do you want to tell me why you did this to me? Isn't it bad enough that you humans have to keep jabbering away at each other all day long?"

She really was talking. Holy hell.

Her voice was somewhat low-pitched, with a definite ironic drawl. Come to think of it, she sounded exactly like—

Well, she sounded just like Janeane Garofalo.

My own voice felt as though it had retreated just then, and, unlike the cat, I didn't know whether I was currently capable of speech. I swallowed, all my nerve endings jangling with shock.

Maybe that second cup of coffee hadn't been such a great idea after all.

"I—" I cleared my throat and went on, "I

wanted you to talk because I know you roam all over downtown, and I was hoping maybe you saw something the night the mayor was killed."

"Don't even know who he is," Tilly replied, with the kind of supreme indifference only a cat could display.

Well, to be fair, she was probably only concerned about the humans who directly impacted her existence, i.e., those of us up and down Bridge Street who fed her and gave her treats and made sure she had fresh water to drink. City Hall was located only a block from the southern edge of Las Vegas's historic downtown, and so I supposed the cat might have ranged that far, but I kind of doubted anyone there would be putting out treats for strays. No, it was much more likely that if anyone saw Tilly lurking in the vicinity, they'd call animal control to scoop up the wandering kitty.

"Tom Gallegos," I said, even though I doubted his name would mean anything to my suddenly loquacious cat. "He was about fifteen years older than me, about so tall"—I paused to raise one hand to indicate a point roughly six inches above my head—"and he had dark hair and dark eyes."

Cats couldn't exactly shrug, but I guessed from the way Tilly's tail twitched that my description hadn't done much to illuminate the mayor's identity for her. "I don't recall," she said.

"Well, did you see anything weird on Saturday night—the night of the harvest festival?" I added, guessing that while the days of the week might not mean much to a cat, an unusual event like the festival would—with any luck—stick out in her memory.

"It was noisy," she said. "Too many people around, so I stayed in the alleyway until they were gone."

I probably should have expected that sort of a reply. A dog might have tried to go and mingle with the crowds, but a cat—especially a cat like Tilly, who was even more independent than most members of the feline tribe—would have wanted to stay as far away as possible.

"You're sure you didn't see anything strange at all?" I persisted. Maybe I should have taken the cat's reply at face value, but since I'd made the leap and cast a spell on her to make her talk, I wasn't quite ready to throw up my hands and walk away.

"I didn't see a damn thing," the cat told me. "I don't know why you keep asking me the same question over and—"

She stopped there, because the back door to the kitchen opened, and Deanne stood there, eyes wide. For a long moment, she stared at Tilly, who'd abruptly shut up the second my friend arrived on the scene, and then she turned her gaze toward me.

"Skye," she said slowly. "Was that—was that cat *talking?*"

Judging by her expression, she was desperately hoping she'd imagined the whole thing—or that maybe she'd walked through a cloud of psychedelics while on her way here from the car.

Denying the whole thing would only delay the inevitable. "Yes," I said wearily. "I cast a spell on her to make her talk."

"You...what?" Deanne managed. Her fingers tightened on the strap of the brown leather purse that hung from one shoulder.

"She cast a spell," Tilly put in. "A really annoying one, too."

"But...but *how?*" Bewildered, my friend looked at the cat again, her brow creasing in a frown. "I mean...you can't *really* do that kind of thing, can you?"

"Apparently, she can," Tilly said. "And now I've proved to you that I didn't see anything suspicious the other night, can you please reverse this stupid spell? I have absolutely no desire to go around chattering all day the way you people do."

Deanne put a hand to her forehead. "I think I need some coffee," she said faintly, and stuffed her purse in a storage cubby before hurrying out into the shop proper.

"Good, she's gone," Tilly said, and tilted her

head in my direction as she gave me a slit-eyed stare. "Now, will you undo the spell?"

"I—well, I'll try," I replied, since I didn't think I should promise anything more than that. A little voice in the back of my head was telling me not to be impulsive, that I really hadn't asked Tilly very many questions, but I quashed it as best I could. Even though the cat obviously wasn't the most cooperative creature in the world, it seemed pretty clear to me she hadn't seen anything of importance. The best thing to do would be to reverse the spell so she could go back to being herself.

It stood to reason that—since all I'd done to create the spell in the first place was to utter a few simple declarative sentences—the only thing I needed to do now was pretty much go through the same procedure all over again, only with the opposite intent.

Magic glowed around my hands as I concentrated once again, and I gathered my thoughts, focusing all my intentions on the cat who sat on the wooden floor a few feet away, her narrowed eyes telling me she was quickly losing patience.

"Tilly, you will no longer have the power of speech. Now you will only make the same sorts of sounds that any other cat would."

A long moment of silence, during which Deanne returned with a mug of coffee held in both hands. In fact, judging by the way her knuckles stood out against the dark green ceramic, it would have taken a crowbar to pry it away.

"Is she—is she still—?"

"Am I still talking?" Tilly interjected, now looking more annoyed than ever. "What do you think?"

Well, damn.

"It should have worked," I said, and Deanne turned puzzled eyes toward me.

"What should have worked?"

"The reversal spell," I explained. "I cast one while you were getting some coffee."

"Well, obviously it didn't," Tilly said. Her tail lashed back and forth, and I had no doubt if she'd been given a human form in addition to human speech, she would have crossed her arms as well...or maybe planted her hands on her hips. "Do something!"

"I *did* do something," I retorted. "Or at least, I thought I did. I'm kind of new to all this magic stuff."

This explanation didn't seem to appease the angry cat. Her eyes narrowed as she said, "If you're that new to it, then maybe you shouldn't have been messing around with something as important as making me talk."

She had a point there. But done was done, so now the only thing I could do was try to fix her predicament somehow.

"I'm sorry," I said. "You just need to give me some more time."

"How much time?" the cat demanded.

I shrugged before I could stop myself. "I'm not sure," I said quickly, hoping the cat hadn't picked up on my utter uncertainty about my ability to perform such a feat. "But I promise I'll figure it out."

Rather than reply directly, Tilly only arched her back and then began to stalk toward the cat door.

Oh, no.

I practically leaped across the room so I could interpose myself between the cat and the little door I'd cut into the wall for her. "You can't leave!" I exclaimed.

"Why not?" the cat demanded.

Deanne came to my rescue. "Because if you say one word to anyone out there"—she made a wild gesture toward the cat door, indicating the wide world beyond the coffee shop—"they'll grab you and send you off to be studied. Do you want to be trapped in a lab...maybe dissected?"

Tilly let out a hiss. Obviously, that particular fate was one she'd prefer to avoid.

"I'm not stupid," the cat said loftily. "I know how to take care of myself."

Considering she'd survived as a stray cat for at

least five or six years, maybe more, I couldn't really argue with that statement. But....

"Okay, you can go out," I said, as Deanne sent me a shocked glance. "On one condition."

Tilly's green eyes turned to slits again. "What condition?"

"You only come to eat here," I told her. "We can't run the risk of you letting something slip after someone gives you a salmon treat, or whatever."

For a moment, the cat was silent as she appeared to consider my terms. "I'll do that," she said, and Deanne and I exchanged a relieved look, "as long as you get me some wet food. Dolores Martinez gives me Blue Buffalo whenever I come by."

The main reason I'd always gotten kibble for Tilly rather than wet cat food was that her visits were so irregular, I couldn't run the risk of leaving something out that would easily spoil. If I were the only one feeding her, though, then that wouldn't be much of an issue.

"Sure," I said, realizing even as I made the promise that the logistics of such a deal were a little more complicated than simply running down to the local Walmart once the morning rush had subsided and getting the cat the food she'd requested. Since I'd been feeding Tilly exclusively Science Diet, it just made sense that I'd get her the same, only in wet food form.

Problem was, none of the local stores carried that brand—I mail-ordered her kibble and treats, which had worked just fine when there wasn't any real urgency involved. Now, though, I realized the closest place to get the food I needed was in Santa Fe, about a forty-minute drive from where we now stood.

I said as much, and Deanne, bless her, jumped right in.

"I can go get it."

As tempting as her offer was, I knew I couldn't spare her for that particular errand. "It's Monday," I pointed out. "You know how busy we are on Monday mornings."

Her face fell. "Oh, right."

Tilly shot me an annoyed glance. "If you can't get me wet food for lunch, the deal's off."

"No, no, it's fine," I said, thinking furiously.

Who did I know who'd be able to drop everything and go running off to Santa Fe on a moment's notice?

An idea sprang into my mind, and I smiled.

"It's okay," I assured her.

"I'll just call Max."

CHAPTER 8

Blame Game

"**Y**ou want me to *what?*" Max asked.

I couldn't really fault him for sounding incredulous, since I knew I probably would have reacted pretty much the same way.

"Can you please go to Santa Fe for me and go to the PetSmart there? It's across the street from the mall, right off Rodeo Road. There's a special kind of cat food I need that I can only get there."

"I didn't know you had a cat."

"I don't," I replied. "I mean, I've been sort of taking care of Tilly, a street cat. But she's suddenly gotten picky and won't eat the kibble I've been feeding her, so I thought I should try some wet food from the same brand."

A long silence. Then he said, "Okay, sure. I don't really have anything going on today, so it's no problem."

Because Tilly had been watching the whole exchange—Deanne was out in the main part of the coffee shop handling the customers, since I'd had to wait until at least a halfway decent hour to call Max —I gave the cat a thumbs-up. Belatedly, I wondered whether she would even understand that very human gesture, but because she seemed to relax a little bit, I had to believe she'd gotten the gist of what I was trying to convey, even if she didn't quite understand all the context.

"You're a godsend, Max," I said, and meant it. "Just bring everything over to the shop when you're done. I'll text you what I need, along with the address to the PetSmart."

"Okay," he said, still sounding a little bemused. To my relief, though, he didn't ask any further questions, only added, "See you in a couple of hours," before hanging up.

"There," I told Tilly as I started composing a quick text to Max, "it's all settled. You'll be set in just a little bit."

"And what am I supposed to do in the mean-time?" the cat inquired.

"Take a nap," I suggested. "I mean, that's what cats do, right?"

That innocent question got me a dagger-sharp stare from my talking feline. "*Some* cats," she said, her tone implying that she definitely shouldn't be lumped in with all those commoners. "It's time for my morning wander."

"Well, I just don't think that's a very good idea right now," I replied. "Can't you make an exception today? Max'll be here in a couple of hours."

Tilly didn't respond right away, and instead let her cool green gaze sweep across the combination kitchen/storeroom that made up the back half of Levitation Latte. To be perfectly honest, it wasn't the world's most inviting place—the space had been designed for utility, not comfort, and had metal racks that held various baking and coffee-brewing supplies, as well as some spare boxes of mugs and serving utensils and other odds and ends, along with the worktable where I did all my mixing and baking, and the big commercial oven that had cost me an arm and a leg.

"I'll have Max get you a bed," I said quickly, and starting to compose an addendum to the text I'd just sent. "And maybe a climbing tree?"

That suggestion got me an insulted stare. "I am not a monkey," Tilly said coldly.

Oops. I supposed I should have realized that cats weren't exactly one size fits all when it came to what amused them. Dooley, the big ginger cat who'd been my grandmother's constant companion and who'd been part of my life since I was a very small child, died only a few months after she passed, leaving me completely alone in the house where I'd grown up. From time to time, I'd thought about getting another cat or maybe even a dog, since my yard was definitely large enough, but since I was gone for such a huge chunk of the day, I decided in the end that getting another pet probably wasn't a very good idea.

Anyway, Dooley had loved his climbing tree and used it pretty much daily right up until the time he died. Still, I shouldn't have presumed that Tilly would be the same way.

"Okay, just a bed," I said hastily. "And some extra salmon treats."

The cat didn't burst out into enthusiastic thank-yous or anything, but at least she inclined her head as she replied, "I guess that'll work."

And then she headed over to the corner where Deanne's and my cubbies were located, curled herself into a ball, and closed her eyes.

Maybe she was asleep or maybe she was just pretending, but it did seem as though she planned to stay put for the moment. I'd thought about stacking a couple of bags of flour in front of the cat door to ensure she wouldn't go out and then decided against taking such an extreme measure. If nothing else, I didn't have a litter box on hand—I'd included one and some kitty litter in my addendum text—because I knew Tilly had always done her business outside while she was roaming around the neighborhood. The last thing I wanted was for her to have an "accident" while I was up front helping customers.

Speaking of which, I'd already spent enough time back here and needed to get out into the shop and take some of the load off Deanne. I'd had to wait until closer to ten to call Max, as I'd guessed that reaching out to him at seven in the morning wasn't a very good idea, so the worst of the morning rush had passed before I slipped back into the storeroom to make the phone call. Even so, we usually got another clot of people between ten and ten-thirty as they took their first break of the day and came out looking for something to sustain them until lunchtime.

To my relief, Deanne wasn't swamped at all when I emerged from the storeroom, but had just finished pouring a go-cup of mocha latte for Will Lassen, who owned an antique store down the street. Once Will was safely out the door, Deanne turned an inquiring gaze toward me.

"So?"

"All handled," I told her as I headed over to the counter and gave the bakery case a quick once-over. Because of all the insanity that morning, I hadn't been able to make a third batch of muffins or any croissants at all, and things were looking pretty depleted. I definitely needed to head into the kitchen and put together some more baked goods, or we were going to be completely out by the time lunch rolled around. "Max is on his way to Santa Fe now."

"Good," she said, and then added, since she'd obviously taken stock of our baked goods as well, "I can keep holding down the fort. You go ahead and get baking, or the natives are really going to get restless."

"Thanks, Deanne," I replied, hoping she could hear how much I truly meant those two words. "I'll be as quick as I can."

And that was why I spent the next hour and a half in the kitchen, whipping together the basics in what felt like record time—another batch of blueberry muffins, some plain and some ham and cheese croissants, a dozen egg bagels just in case someone wanted one to nosh on at lunch. It wasn't quite my usual spread, but I hoped it would be enough to hold us until closing time rolled around at three-thirty.

I'd just finished sliding the last of the bagels into the display case when Max appeared, hauling several oversized shopping bags with him. "Beware Greeks bearing gifts," he announced, and then paused a few feet away from the counter, as though unsure as to what he was supposed to do with all the loot he'd brought for me.

Once again, I sent a pleading glance in Deanne's direction. She only shook her head, saying, "Go on. I can watch everything up here for now. Just try to be back before the lunch hordes start to appear."

I assured her I wouldn't leave her in the lurch, and then told Max, "Come on back to the kitchen."

Looking puzzled but game, he followed me through the shop's public area and back to the space where Tilly was still sleeping, curled up in the corner. Maybe she'd gone out to do her business while I was baking and getting everything set out in the display case, but if she had, at least she'd come right back inside.

"What's all this about, anyway?" he asked, then glanced over at the sleeping feline. "Is it for that cat?"

At once, her green eyes opened, and she gave my companion a contemptuous glance. "Yeah, I'm 'that' cat."

I supposed Max could be forgiven for looking just a little gobsmacked. He took a step backward, bright blue eyes wide as he stared down at the black ball of fur. "Did—did that cat just *talk?*"

"Yes," I said wearily, even as Tilly put in,

"I did—and I have to tell you, this whole talking thing is kind of exhausting."

After delivering that remark, she curled up again, only this time with her head practically in the corner, in what seemed to me an obvious move to block out as much of Max's and my conversation as possible.

He glanced over at me, still obviously off balance. "Skye, what the hell is going on?"

I let out a breath. "Well, I guess you could say it's my fault. I cast a spell on Tilly to make her talk, but I honestly thought I'd be able to reverse it."

Max still wore the expression of a man who'd just seen a unicorn walking down the middle of Bridge Street. "You 'cast a spell'?" he repeated. "I thought you didn't do that kind of thing."

"Well, I don't," I replied. "Or at least, I didn't." I paused there and slanted a narrow-eyed glance up at him. "Actually, I think some of this is your fault, too."

"*My* fault?" he said, looking more incredulous than ever. "What the heck did I have to do with any of it?"

Maybe I should have been a little more diplomatic. However, since I'd already put my foot in it, I figured I might as well plow ahead.

"You're the one who told me I should do more with my magic," I argued. "And you're the one who said I should practice more. So"—I paused to incline my head toward the supposedly sleeping cat in the corner—"this is the result."

"You're seriously blaming this on me?" Max shot back.

The last thing I wanted was to get into a full-on confrontation with Max Sullivan. I already had enough on my plate. I released a breath and said, "Okay, not really. But I surfed around on YouTube last night and found this woman who was demonstrating how to 'release the magic within,' and so I followed her lead and made a bunch of gourds dance around above the dining room table."

He blinked. "How did you manage to do that?"

"I don't know, exactly," I replied. "I just concentrated and focused on my magic, and then...."

The words trailed off, since I'd been focusing on doing that very thing even as I spoke. This time, it felt a little easier to connect with the magic inside me, as though, because I'd done this a couple of times already, I was getting more confident in my ability to reach within and wake up those sleeping gifts.

Once again, that glittery, glowing light sprang forth from my fingertips. However, since I wasn't chanting a spell, it didn't have anywhere to go, and therefore only began to twine itself around me as Max stood a few feet away and stared in amazement.

"That's...that's magic?" he asked in hushed tones.

"I guess so," I said. "At least, that's what

happens when I reach inside and really try to wake it up. And then I can have it do things like this."

As I spoke, I envisioned the magic rising up to one of the shelves and lifting a pack of paper napkins and a container of stir sticks. At once, the two cardboard packages rose from their respective shelves, floated above our heads, and then did a little midair twirl before returning to their original positions.

"That's amazing," Max breathed...after he'd recovered himself enough to have regained the power of speech. "You cast a spell to do that?"

"Not exactly," I replied after pausing for a second or two to consider his question. "I mean, I just sort of imagined what I wanted to happen... and then it did."

Once again, he was silent for a moment. Then he asked, "Did you do that when you got the cat to talk?"

I shook my head. "No, I cast a real spell to make her speak." Thoughts churning, I said, "Do you think that's the problem? That I cast a spell instead of just imagining Tilly talking?"

Max spread his hands, looking singularly help-less. "I have absolutely no idea. I mean, before right now, I couldn't have imagined anything like this was even possible."

Those words made me lift an eyebrow. "But there you were, telling me I should practice my magic and get better at it. Were you just blowing smoke or something?"

A hint of color showed beneath his apparently perpetual tan. I had to wonder if he would still look that way when winter rolled around, since Las Vegas, New Mexico, was kind of short on tanning salons.

"No, I wasn't 'blowing smoke,'" he told me. "I was only thinking of the way you read tea leaves, and how if you really worked at it, you could get a little more accurate."

That comment didn't win him any points. "I *am* accurate," I said, the words coming out a little more annoyed than I'd planned. "Like I told you before, I'm almost eighty-percent accurate. There isn't a whole lot of room for improvement there."

At least he had the courtesy to appear almost abashed. "Okay, that came out wrong. It's just...." He stopped there, as though he wasn't quite sure what he'd meant to say. "I guess I really wasn't thinking it all the way through. I definitely wasn't imagining anything like this." A wave toward the packages of napkins and stirrers, now quiescent on their shelves, although I noticed he didn't gesture at Tilly.

Maybe he wanted to let sleeping cats lie.

"Why *did* you make her talk, anyway?" he asked.

I chose to ignore the abrupt shift in topic. It

seemed that Max had once again leaped before he looked, and now he wasn't quite sure what to do about the aftermath of him shooting off his mouth and giving me such disastrous advice.

Not that I really could blame him for any of this, as much as I might have liked to. Maybe he'd been talking about something he didn't understand, but he wasn't the one who'd encouraged me to watch that Madame Wanda video and follow her steps for "awakening the magic within," and he certainly hadn't held a gun to my head as I chanted that stupid incantation to make Tilly talk.

"I thought she might have seen something," I told him. "You know, on the night Tom Gallegos was murdered. She's always wandering around Bridge Street and the park."

At once, Max's expression shifted, his blue eye bright with interest. "Did she?"

"Not a darn thing," I replied in disgust. "She said she stayed away from the festival because it was too noisy."

To my surprise, he didn't seem overly disappointed by this particular revelation. "Well, just because she didn't see anything at the festival, that doesn't mean she might not still be helpful."

Not sure what he was getting at, I replied dubiously, "Helpful how?"

He glanced over at the cat. Since her back was to us, it was hard to tell whether she was really asleep or not. However, he didn't appear to be too worried about Tilly's current state of unconsciousness, because he said, "Well, you said she's always roaming around downtown. She might hear something or see something now that she knows what to look for."

"Like what?" I asked. I thought I could see where Max was going with this, but I didn't know whether I was on board with the plan.

"Anything suspicious," he said.

"You might need to be a little more precise about that," I told him. "Just because someone is acting sketchy doesn't mean they were involved in the mayor's murder."

I got an off-hand lift of the shoulders in response to my comment. "We don't need to ask that much of her," Max replied. "We just need her to report whatever she sees, and then we can be the ones to analyze it and see whether it's connected to the murder or not." A pause, and then he added triumphantly, "She can be our feline spy."

CHAPTER 9

Cata Hari

"Oh, hell no," Tilly broke in, rousing from her supposed "sleep" so she could face the two of us, ears flattened and wearing an expression of equal alarm and disdain. "No self-respecting cat would fetch and carry for a couple of humans."

"We're not asking you to 'fetch and carry,'" Max replied, his tone reasonable. If he was experiencing any cognitive dissonance at carrying on a conversation with a cat, you'd never know it to look at him. Then again, Max always had been the type to roll with the punches. "All we want is for you to tell Skye if you notice anything that doesn't feel right, that seems out of the ordinary."

"After all," I added, since I could tell from the cat's continued hostile expression that she didn't want any part of our schemes, "you spend most of your time out and about downtown anyway. It's not like I expect you to change much about your habits. I just want you to let me know if you see something fishy."

"'Fishy,'" the cat repeated in a very different tone. "I only wish there were lots of fish around here. But that's the problem with living in a desert."

I almost corrected her that Las Vegas was located in a high desert chaparral region, not the Sahara. But since I figured it was better not to get sidetracked, I let the snarky comment go.

"It's really not a big deal," I said.

The cat stared at me for a moment. "It's a big deal to me," she replied. "Just like having to talk to you like this. It's exhausting."

Max glanced over at me, and I gave a very slight lift of my shoulders. Honestly, I was already bribing the cat with canned food and extra treats just to make sure she kept her mouth shut around anyone who wasn't part of our little group who already knew her secret. Because of that, I didn't have a whole heck of a lot left to offer her.

I should have known Max Sullivan would put his foot in it.

"Well, you do this for us, and Skye will make sure you won't have to talk like this anymore."

Great. Just great.

Tilly slid her green-hued gaze toward me. "You will?"

"No," I said at once, even as Max's eyes flared in alarm. Clearly, he'd thought it would be okay to tell the cat a few white lies if it meant we could convince her to act as our spy. "I mean," I went on hastily as her tail began to twitch in irritation, "I'll do my best. But I'm new to this whole magic thing, so I'm not going to make promises I can't keep."

An odd expression passed over Tilly's feline features.

Was that grudging respect?

"All right," she said after a long pause. "I suppose I'll have to be okay with that. Better tell your man there to keep his nose out of places where it doesn't belong."

My mouth opened to tell her that Max wasn't "my" man—as much as I might have liked him to be—but then I shut it again. Being a cat, she probably wouldn't care about the subtle distinction that while Max might be my friend, he definitely wasn't my guy.

Luckily, he didn't look too offended by the cat's remark. Maybe he was realizing that he'd already overstepped his bounds and therefore should stay out of any further exchanges between Tilly and me.

"I think he's learned his lesson," I said solemnly.

Another long silence, and then Tilly's little

black nose wiggled a bit. "I'll keep an eye out...but I won't promise anything."

I sent her a grateful smile. "That's all anyone could ask for."

Max left soon after that, since it was getting close to noon and I knew I needed to be back out front to help Deanne with the lunch rush. However, his eyes were still full of questions, and he put his thumb and pinky finger to his ear and mouth as he went out, indicating that he planned to call me later when I wasn't so busy.

Under normal circumstances, I would have been thrilled beyond belief that he wanted to get in touch so soon after seeing me in person. However, this time I knew he just wanted to pick my brain a little more about how I'd managed to make a stray cat sound like she'd been possessed by a disaffected Gen X comedian.

Deanne also sent me a questioning glance as I hurried behind the counter, but about all I could say was, "It's handled," before several people I'd never seen before, probably tourists, approached and placed an order for a couple of iced coffees.

After that, we both had our hands full as more and more people came in, some only wanting to supplement a sandwich they'd bought elsewhere with a latte or maybe an espresso if they were feeling particularly sluggish that Monday afternoon. By the time one-thirty rolled around, all the croissants and bagels I'd made earlier were gone, and we only had about a dozen muffins left.

Tough call. Dealing with Tilly had made me more tired than I wanted to admit, and I really didn't feel like baking anything else that day, especially since some of it was sure to still be left on the bakery case's shelves when it came time to close.

It's not the end of the world if we run out, I told myself. *If nothing else, it'll let people know they shouldn't wait too long if they want to get a muffin on any particular day.*

With that thorny problem settled, I slipped out from behind the counter and went back to the kitchen to check on the cat.

She wasn't there.

Alarm flared, but I tamped it down as best I could. After all, this was the deal we'd both agreed to. I'd ensure she got the food and treats she wanted, and in return, she'd keep her mouth shut as she made the rounds on Bridge Street and its environs. Even if she was tempted to talk to one of the people who usually fed her, she was smart enough to realize attracting that sort of attention was the last thing she would want.

Still, I fretted about what to do if she didn't return by the time Deanne and I were done closing up the coffee shop. The cat and I hadn't discussed what she intended to do during the overnight hours, but it seemed logical to me that she'd need to come and stay at my place. And all right, that particular arrangement hadn't worked out so well the first time I'd tried it, but that had been several years earlier.

A lot had changed since then.

"Everything all right?" Deanne asked when I came back out to the main part of the shop.

"I don't know," I said. "Tilly's not there."

At once, an expression of extreme concern passed over my friend's features. "I thought the whole deal was that she needed to stay put."

"Well, it was more that she needed to keep her mouth shut," I replied. "I knew she wouldn't cooperate at all if I tried to keep her locked up in the back room. But I'm not sure what I should do if she isn't here when it's time for us to leave."

Deanne glanced toward the front window, then back over at me. It was the dead time of the afternoon, post-lunch but before we got a minor influx of high school kids on their way home from school, looking for any leftover muffins and maybe getting a mochaccino or an iced tea to fuel that day's homework. "Do you want to go out and look for her?"

I shook my head. "No, that's all right. I doubt I'd even be able to track her down. If she's not here when I want to go home, I'll just hang around a bit and see if she surfaces."

That notion didn't seem to sit very well with my friend, since she frowned slightly at the suggestion. "I can stay, too, if you want."

"No, it's fine," I said at once. Deanne already worked a crazy enough schedule on my behalf; the last thing I wanted was for her to stick around after she'd put in her eight hours, especially since I'd left her on her own today for way too long while I was dealing with my magical cat problem.

"If you're sure—"

"I'm sure," I said firmly. "Besides, it's not as though Tilly will be locked out even if we're not here. She's been coming and going through that cat door just fine for the past couple of years."

This common-sense evaluation of the situation seemed to reassure Deanne, because she didn't raise any further objections, only nodded and then picked up a damp rag before heading over to a table that needed to be wiped down.

And we did end up having enough late afternoon traffic to completely wipe out the contents of the bakery case and keep us busy until it was finally time to turn around the sign in the front window, letting the world know that Levitation Latte was closed until 7 a.m. the next day.

Still no sign of Tilly, though. Deanne and I went through our usual closing-up routine, making sure all the coffee carafes were thoroughly cleaned out and drying on the rack on the counter and the espresso machine was likewise cleaned and ready for the next day. The dishwasher hummed with plates and mugs being washed, and all the tabletops were spotless.

And still no cat.

"Go ahead and go home," I told Deanne, who still seemed inclined to linger even though I'd told her I didn't expect her to stick around. "I'll wait for another ten minutes or so, but after that, Tilly's on her own."

Deanne didn't seem too thrilled by these developments, but she didn't argue with me, only said she hoped the cat would show up soon, and then got her purse and headed out to her car.

Even though we always tidied up after we closed for the day, there were a few things I knew I could do to waste some time in the hope that Tilly might eventually appear. I refilled the sugar and cinnamon shakers, and went out into the coffee shop's main area so I could make sure the chairs were set at perfect ninety-degree angles to one another at each table.

Probably, no one except me cared about those sorts of things, but I thought they made Levitation Latte look a little more pulled together.

However, all those little tasks only took me about ten minutes or so. By that point, it was nearly four o'clock, and I had a decision to make. Either I could stay here and whip up the batter for the next morning's muffins and stick it in the fridge, or I could just say the hell with it and head home. That meant I'd need to come back in an hour or so to see if Tilly had decided to make an appearance, but I always started to get antsy when I was stuck at the shop too long past closing.

Batter it was.

However, I'd just set the dry ingredients on the kitchen counter when I heard the distinctive *smack* of the cat door closing. At once, I turned around.

Tilly had gone straight to her bowl of water in the storage section of the back room and was lapping at it in a leisurely way that seemed to suggest she didn't have a care in the world. I set my hands on my hips and scowled down at her.

"Where've you been?"

One ear flattened slightly, but otherwise, she didn't appear to give any indication that she'd heard my question. Only after she'd finished drinking did she bother to turn around.

"I was out wandering, just like I said I would be."

"Well, you know the shop closes at three-thirty. I—"

"No, I don't know that," she cut in. "You think cats care about clocks and time? I came back when I was ready to."

On the surface, that sounded like a valid argument. However, considering that Dooley, my grandmother's cat, had known exactly when his mealtimes were and complained vociferously if they were even a few minutes late, I wasn't buying it.

"Sure," I said, although I wasn't going to push it any more than that. My truce with Tilly was a fragile one, and I didn't want to do anything that might shatter it. "Well, I'm glad you're here now. We need to get going."

At once, her ears swiveled and her eyes narrowed. "Going where?"

"To my house," I told her. "I can't leave you here alone all night."

"Why not?" she demanded. "You've been doing that very thing for years."

All right, she had a point there. Even so, to say circumstances had recently changed would be an understatement.

"You didn't talk back then," I said.

Her whiskers twitched. "And? You just let me roam around all afternoon by myself. What difference does it make if I'm here alone at night?"

Once again, I wasn't sure of the best way to counter her argument. On the surface, she was making perfect sense. But....

Before I could say anything, she went on, "You tried taking me to your house a while back. That little experiment didn't turn out so great, if I recall correctly."

No, it hadn't. She'd meowed and whined all night, scratching at the front door to be let out. Of course, there was no way in the world I would have allowed her to roam around a neighborhood she didn't know, so I'd suffered the lack of sleep and then had promptly returned her to her familiar haunts the next morning.

"Still," I said, and paused. What with everything that was going on, I really didn't feel like living through another sleepless night just because of a cranky cat.

"'Still' nothing," she said. "I'll be fine. Who knows? Maybe I'll see something important. Don't you humans do a lot of your dirty work at night?"

Okay, she had me there. Honestly, it was in Tilly's best interests for her to fly below the radar. She seemed to understand what would happen if anyone outside our little group heard her talking, and so I knew that I needed to trust her now to take care of herself.

I couldn't help being a little worried, though. The cat obviously knew how to take care of herself, or she wouldn't have survived on the street for so long, and yet she couldn't exactly call or text if something did go wrong.

"I guess they do," I said. "Just...be careful, okay?"

She sniffed again. "I'm always careful," she replied, and then stalked over to the bed Max had bought her in Santa Fe and curled herself into a small black ball in the corner.

That appeared to be my signal to leave. Since I knew she was here for the moment, I went ahead and opened a can of roasted chicken and rice cat food and scooped it into her bowl, then rinsed off the spoon before letting myself out.

Just as I was about to back out of my parking space behind the building, my phone rang. At once, I scooped it out of my purse and looked down at the screen.

Max.

"Hey," I said, putting the phone up to my right ear with one hand as I attempted to fasten my seat-belt with the other. "What's up?"

"How's our enchanted kitty?"

"Just fine," I replied. "She just got in from wandering around this afternoon, so I gave her some dinner and am about to head home."

"You're leaving her alone there?"

His tone wasn't quite accusatory enough for me to take offense...especially since I'd just been arguing with the cat over that very thing only a few minutes earlier.

"She insisted," I said. "Anyway, she knows what side her bread is buttered on, so I think it will be fine."

"Okay," he replied. "And hey—I was calling to see if you wanted to come over. Lou made some of his killer marinara sauce, and there's tons of it. Please say you'll help me eat it so I won't be swimming in sauce for the next week."

He sounded so plaintive, I just had to smile. And while it was also amusing that one of his bodyguards had turned out to be something of a chef, I definitely wasn't going to turn down Max's invitation.

After my little adventure in magic the night before, I thought it was probably a good idea not to be left to my own devices.

"On my way," I said. "Anything you want me stop and get?"

"Nope," he said cheerfully. "Lou also made bread, so I think we're good."

Normally, I was leery about eating anyone else's baked goods, since my own muffins and rolls and croissants had pretty much spoiled me for anything else. But since I'd had the good fortune to try one of Lou's baguettes a week earlier, I knew he was the real deal. Why the guy was working as a bodyguard rather than running a restaurant somewhere, I didn't know.

Actually, I thought I probably did. The money and the hours in Max's employ were probably a lot better than they would have been working in the food service industry.

So I pointed my Subaru east and crossed over I-25, heading toward the sprawling ranch that Max had made his home away from Hollywood. As far as I knew, he hadn't sold his house in Bel-Air, and wasn't planning to rent it out. It sounded as though his assistant stayed there just enough to keep the place from being empty all the time, and the arrangement appeared to suit both of them just fine. Once or twice I'd asked him if she ever planned to come to Las Vegas, and he'd immediately shaken his head.

"No, I don't think our part of the world would suit Courtney very well," he told me. "Besides, we get along just fine with our Zoom calls and emails and whatever else we need to do to stay in contact. There's really no reason for her to come out here."

Which in a way, had suited me just fine. Not that I could probably look at her as a rival, but still, she'd been working with Max for the past six years and knew way more about his life than I did.

Al was manning the gate as I drove up, and he waved me in with a smile. He didn't seem to be as multi-talented as Lou, but he was certainly pretty friendly for a bodyguard.

Or maybe it was more that he knew exactly who I was, and also knew I didn't pose any kind of a threat to his boss.

I parked in front of the garage, slung my purse over one shoulder—unlike Deanne, who seemed to carry half her worldly belongings in her bag, my own purse was a minimal affair that held my phone, wallet, a tube of lip gloss, and not much else —and headed for the door. At this time of year, the trees planted around the house shimmered with autumn gold, and, not for the first time, I thought of what a beautiful spot this truly was. Max had definitely ended up in one of Las Vegas's premier locations.

Which shouldn't have surprised me at all. He might not have been a cat, but he certainly knew how to land on his feet.

Almost as soon as I rang the doorbell, the door opened, and he smiled down at me. "That was fast."

"Well, it's not like we have a lot of traffic around here."

"True."

He stepped aside to let me in. Almost at once, the warm aroma of marinara and fresh-baked bread met my nose, and I let out a happy little sigh.

"That smells amazing," I said, and glanced around. As far as I could tell, Max and I appeared to be alone in the house...although, to be fair, the place was big enough that Lou could have been at the far end or even out on one of the patios. "Where's the chef?"

"Oh, he headed home after Al showed up," Max said, leading me along the short corridor that opened into the family room. "There's no reason for both of them to be hanging around all the time these days, since the paparazzi have apparently decided I'm too boring to stalk."

I had to smile at that remark. In the days that followed Evan Bryant's arrest, Las Vegas was still thick with celebrity photographers trying to catch a glimpse of Max as he did his best to settle into something resembling a normal life. As time went on, though, they dropped away one by one, obviously deciding that the public only needed so many shots of him emerging from the local Walgreens, or whatever. In fact, he probably didn't require Al or Lou's services at all, since the ranch had a state-of-the-art security system with cameras everywhere.

For whatever reason, though, he'd kept them on, and I honestly found myself comforted by that fact. Better to play it safe than get caught off guard...and if Max got to avail himself of Lou's cooking in the meantime, all the better.

"I didn't know you Hollywood types ate so early," I quipped, and he shot me a pained glance.

"Well, I was kind of hoping we could wait until at least six," he said. "The sauce is keeping warm on the stove, and Lou wrapped up the bread and promised me it would still be fresh when we sat down to eat at a more civilized time."

"That works," I replied, even as I wondered

what he planned to do with the intervening time, since it was only a little past four-thirty.

But after he'd poured some water for the two of us—apparently guessing it probably wasn't a good idea to start drinking quite so soon—his intentions became clear enough. "Can you show me the video you watched last night?" he asked as he picked up the remote for his Apple TV.

"Um...sure," I said. I didn't really know what watching it again would prove, but since I was more than happy to spend as much time in Max's company as possible, I wasn't going to argue. "Just search for 'Madame Wanda.' It should be easy to find her channel."

Sure enough, he located the channel in question right away, and then scrolled down to her playlists, of which there were at least ten. "Do you know which one it's in?"

I shook my head. "No—I was just surfing around and found the video that way. But"—I paused to scan the titles of the various playlists, hoping one of them would jump out as the most likely place for the video I'd watched to be located —"try the playlist called 'Empower Yourself.'"

While that seemed like the logical place for the video to be, it turned out the titles there all appeared to be your usual self-help kind of stuff. After bouncing around from playlist to playlist for a couple of minutes, Max paused and looked over at me.

"'Awakening the Magic Within'?"

"That's the one."

He hit the play button and let the video roll. Watching it, I felt the slightest embarrassed flush rise in my cheeks. After all, it was one thing to watch something like this on my own when I was desperately trying to find some answers, and quite another to have Max sitting there on the other side of the sectional, face impassive as Madame Wanda waved her hands and spoke in sepulchral tones of the magic sleeping inside every one of us. As if for the first time, I noticed how cheesy her backdrop of painted moons and stars actually looked, and how the glittering rings on her fingers were obviously fake.

And yet....

And yet, something she'd said had struck a chord, had made me reach inside for the magic sleeping there. Maybe I could have imagined those flying gourds the night before, but I had Max and Deanne as witnesses to the somewhat stupefying reality of Tilly the Talking Cat. That wasn't my imagination.

No, that was real.

Throughout the whole video, Max didn't utter a word, but only sat there and watched with the quiet intensity of someone attending a philosophy lecture. When it was done, he stopped the playback before it could roll over to the next video, then set the remote down on the coffee table.

"You think she's the real deal?" he asked.

To my relief, there wasn't any scorn in his voice, only what sounded like natural curiosity.

"I don't know," I confessed. "I mean, she really doesn't look like it, does she? But the things she's telling people to do in that video seemed to work for me."

"I'd say it's more than just 'seemed,'" he said dryly, "considering I had a conversation with a cat earlier today. Speaking of which, you really think she's okay being left alone?"

"That's what she wanted," I replied. "And I thought it was better not to push it." I stopped there and looked back over at the TV screen. "I have to wonder...do you think anyone else has used Madame Wanda's techniques to really practice magic?"

"I doubt it," Max said. "Otherwise, we'd be knee-deep in talking cats and flying vegetables and God knows what else."

"Gourds," I corrected him, and he grinned.

"Whatever. I guess the next trick is trying to figure out if these new powers of yours can help with tracking down who killed the mayor."

The whole time, I'd been holding a glass of water in one hand. I set it down now and sent Max a quizzical look. "I thought that's what we were using Tilly for."

He didn't blink. "Well, that's one part of the plan," he said. "But it would be kind of stupid not use your own powers to work on the problem, too."

"So...what?" I asked. "You expect me to bust out a Ouija board and see if we can communicate with Tom that way, ask him if he can tell us who killed him?"

Max's blue eyes glinted at me. "Would that work?"

Damn. I really hadn't expected him to take my words at face value. "I don't know," I said. "I don't even own a Ouija board."

"That's all right," he said at once. "I don't think you really need something like that. We could just use a piece of card stock with 'yes' and 'no' and the letters of the alphabet written on it, couldn't we?"

In theory, I supposed something like that would work. However....

"You seriously want to have a séance," I said slowly, while at the same time wondering how I could ask him to abandon this dubious plan. Not likely; Max could be like a dog with a bone when he latched on to something.

"Sure, why not?"

"Because I'm not a medium," I pointed out. "I

don't know the first thing about communing with the spirits of the dead, or whatever."

Now he just grinned. "Have you ever tried?"

Of course I hadn't. Or rather, while I'd tried reaching out to the ghost of my Grandmother Maureen in the weeks following her death, mostly because I was alone and scared and didn't know what I should do next, I'd never heard from her. In a way, I was almost glad. If she'd been hanging around on this plane, that would have indicated she had unfinished business of some kind. Her complete radio silence seemed to be a signal that she'd moved on and was happy wherever she was.

Or it could all be a lot of hooey. I couldn't really deny magic existed, not after what I'd experienced during the past twenty-four hours, but I didn't know for sure whether I was ready to admit to the reality of an afterlife.

"Unless you're talking about Deanne and me playing 'Bloody Mary in the mirror' during a sleepover or something, then no, I haven't."

Being Max, he didn't seem at all deterred by any of this. "That's fine," he said. "It's obvious you're connected to magic and to other planes, or you wouldn't be able to read tea leaves and have dreams that come true. We just need to put together a small séance—maybe you and me and Deanne and Mike—and then we can see if we can get some answers out of Tom Gallegos."

Oh, I could just imagine Deanne's reaction if I asked her to participate in a séance. She had absolutely no issues with my fortune-telling abilities, but she was still a pretty staunch churchgoer, the kind of person who might throw some serious side-eye at the suggestion that we should commune with the spirits of the dead in order to ask the mayor exactly who'd slipped that rope around his neck and then dumped his body in the corn maze.

Problem was, I didn't really know who else to ask. I had lots of acquaintances in town, but true friends were much thinner on the ground. Even though plenty of years had passed, I still had a hard time trusting anyone who'd teased me—or worse—during my school years. No doubt Kyle Isaacs would be all too happy to help me out, no matter what his personal feelings about séances, but the last thing I wanted was to have him and Max in the same room, mostly because I didn't want Kyle observing our interactions and maybe putting two and two together.

"Go ahead and give her a call," Max urged me. "You won't know unless you ask."

Because I guessed he would keep pestering me until I gave in, I went ahead and got my phone out of my purse, then entered Deanne's phone number. A moment later, she picked up and said, "Skye?"

She sounded puzzled, and I couldn't really

blame her. Usually, I didn't call her right away after work unless something strange had popped up.

Well, in this particular case, I supposed that was only the truth.

"Hey," I said. "I know this is going to sound a little weird, but would you and Mike be up for getting together with me and Max tomorrow night for a séance?"

"A what?" she replied.

Might as well lay it all out there. "He wants to try getting in touch with Tom Gallegos' ghost."

A long pause. Then she asked, "Do you really think that'll work?"

"I don't know," I said. "But we should probably give it a try."

She went quiet again. "Okay," she responded at length. "We don't have any plans for tomorrow, so...sure, why not? Where do you want to get together?"

I glanced over at Max. "Where should we have the séance?"

"Here," he said at once. "I can get Lou to make pizza for all of us."

Somehow, I doubted that cooking for guests had been part of Lou's contract, but that was between him and Max. Anyway, it seemed as though the bodyguard really liked to cook, so I wasn't going to argue.

"Here at Max's," I told Deanne. "Say...six-thirty? He's going to feed us all dinner."

"Sounds great," she said, her voice now positively excited. "I've been dying to see inside Max's house. I'll let Mike know." No mention of asking whether her husband would be okay with attending a séance, mostly because Mike went along with pretty much anything Deanne suggested, especially if it involved free food.

"Okay. See you tomorrow morning."

"See you."

I ended the call and slid my phone back into my purse, then glanced over at Max. "It's a go."

"Great," he said. "I just know we're going to get the answers we need."

About all I could do was smile wanly at him.

He seemed sure I could deliver Tom Gallegos' ghost on a platter...but I doubted it would be that easy.

CHAPTER 10

Medium Undone

The next morning, Deanne was practically brimming with excitement. "Oh, this is going to be so cool!" she exclaimed after we'd said our customary good mornings and I'd handed her a mug of French roast. "I've never been to a séance before. What should I wear?"

That particular question hadn't even crossed my mind. Sure, I'd already made mental plans to get cleaned up and freshen my face before I headed over to Max's house that night, but the concept of special clothes for a séance definitely hadn't entered the equation.

"I don't know," I said. "A clean shirt?"

She made a face. "That doesn't sound very respectful. I was thinking maybe that black dress I wore to Mike's grandfather's funeral. It's kind of flowy, sort of Stevie Nicks."

Since I hadn't seen the dress in question, I'd have to take my friend's word for it. "I'm kind of short on Stevie Nicks–inspired pieces in my wardrobe."

Deanne shook her head. "Maybe, but you have that dress you bought in Santa Fe last fall. Have you worn it even once?"

No, I hadn't, mostly because the right sort of occasion had never presented itself. It was a sort of slinky knit in a dark, smoky purple with a crossover bodice and a flared skirt, and looked pretty spectacular on. Even now, I couldn't exactly say why I'd bought the piece in the first place, since I hadn't been dating anyone at the time and certainly didn't have any events coming up where I would have needed to wear something like that. But the dress had called to me, for whatever reason, and so I'd brought it home, figuring it was classic enough in cut that I should be able to get some decent wear out of it, even if it ended up hanging in my closet for months...which was pretty much exactly what had happened.

I shook my head, and she said, "Then you have to wear it. Luckily, Mike's work clothes should be good enough, so I'll just make sure he doesn't change when he gets home this afternoon."

Good thing Mike was such an easy-going guy. He'd do just about anything to make Deanne happy, up to and including attending a séance...and staying in the dress slacks and button-up shirt from his job in the city's community development department rather than changing into the jeans and T-shirts he preferred when hanging around the house.

And she just loved to get dressed up, which didn't happen much in a place like Las Vegas...especially when your 9-5 involved working in a coffee shop.

"Sounds like we're set," I said. "I'd better text Max to warn him, though."

Which I did, although I waited until a slightly more decent hour to do so. *Deanne thinks we need to show proper respect for the dead, so she's expecting us all to dress for the occasion. Just wanted to give you a heads-up.*

No problem, he wrote back. *I'll dust off one of my tuxes.*

I had no doubt that Max owned several tuxedos, considering all the awards shows he'd attended over the years. However, I kind of doubted he'd brought any of them with him to Las Vegas. It wasn't exactly a black tie kind of place.

Rather than point out that obvious fact, I only sent him a tongue-out emoji, and he responded by telling me, *See you all at 6:30.*

Well, at least I hadn't scared him into backing out of the whole deal.

Nothing much of note happened that morning

—Tilly had kept her word and clearly stayed in all night, although she was out the door as soon as I gave her the all-clear—but I was okay with that. A little peaceful routine...or not so peaceful, considering how busy we were...was just what I needed to get myself back on track. Yes, I'd made a cat talk, and was going to lead a séance this evening, but in the meantime, I wanted to pretend everything was completely normal.

A little after one o'clock, Cory Sills came into the shop. She looked pale and wan, which I didn't find too strange, considering her boss had been found dead just a couple of days before. Tucked under one arm was a stack of what looked like pale blue flyers.

She caught sight of me—Deanne was in the back, doing inventory during the post-lunch slow-down—and headed right for the counter. "Hi, Skye," she said.

"Hi, Cory," I replied. "How're you holding up?"

A small lift of her shoulders. "Okay, I guess. It's been...a little crazy."

I could imagine. My gaze moved toward the stack of flyers she'd brought with her. "What are those?"

She immediately pulled a piece of paper from the top of the stack and handed it over to me. "There's going to be a meeting tomorrow night at

City Hall. Anyone who wants to run for mayor in the special election has to show up and declare their candidacy so they can get on the ballot for the election next Tuesday."

My eyes widened a bit at her explanation. Sure, I'd guessed there would have to be an election of some sort to fill the empty position, but I didn't think it would happen so quickly. In the interim, Alex Donnelly, the deputy mayor, was holding down the fort, although even I knew it wasn't as though he'd automatically assume Tom Gallegos' seat. No, the mayor position had to be put up for a vote—a very quick vote, apparently.

"I was hoping you could put the flyer in your front window," Cory went on. "We sent an email blast about the meeting, but I'm also asking as many local merchants as possible to post these someplace public so we can get the word out that way, too. Not everyone has email."

Or checked it if they did. My usual habit was to look at my email first thing in the morning or late in the afternoon after I got home from work, but I didn't stick to that routine with any regularity. Most of my important business was handled via text.

However, I knew City Hall hadn't modernized enough to use texts as its preferred form of communication, and so it had to fall back on email. This wasn't a lot of notice, but having the flyer up in the front window would definitely help spread the word.

"Of course I will," I assured Cory as I briefly scanned the flyer. It was pretty basic, just a few quick lines to inform people that anyone wishing to declare their candidacy needed to be at City Hall at seven-thirty on Wednesday, October nineteenth, and that the special election would be held on Tuesday, October twenty-fifth. Hoping I didn't sound too dubious, I asked, "Isn't this happening pretty fast?"

"It is," she replied, unruffled. "But it's written into the city charter that any special elections to fill a vacancy in city government have to take place within ten days of the vacancy occurring. We could have pushed it back a couple of days, but why?"

No good reason, I supposed. It wasn't as though there would be hundreds of candidates vying for the spot Tom Gallegos' unexpected death had left open. I assumed Alex Donnelly would run —and most likely win. He wasn't exactly the world's most charismatic person...he owned a local accounting firm...but at least everyone could depend on him to be competent. And maybe there would be one or two other people who were inter- ested in becoming mayor, which I assumed was the reason for the meeting tomorrow night.

"I'll let as many people know as I can," I promised her, and she sent me a relieved smile.

"Thanks so much, Skye," she said. "That'll really help."

Cory left after that, stack of flyers still tucked under one arm. Just as the door was swinging shut behind her, Deanne emerged from the storeroom and blinked as the woman's shadow passed by the shop windows.

"Was that Cory Sills?"

I nodded. "Yep. I guess they're having a meeting tomorrow night for anyone who wants to throw their hat into the ring as the next mayor."

Deanne's nose wrinkled. "Talk about moving on before the body's even cold."

She had kind of a point there. As far as I knew, Tom's funeral hadn't been scheduled yet, possibly because the family was waiting to get his body back from the medical examiner's office. No one had said anything to me on the subject, and I wasn't going to ask. It wasn't as though I'd been close enough to Tom—or anyone else in the family— that I could reasonably be expected to attend his services.

Well, maybe Kyle would drop in and provide some much-needed information on that particular topic. His visits tended to be fraught, since I never knew when he was going to try asking me out again, but I couldn't deny that he was a useful source of information.

Unfortunately, he didn't make an appearance

that day, telling me he was either super-busy...
which I found hard to believe, since Las Vegas
wasn't exactly seething with crime on its worst
day...or he had the day off and was filling it with
more amusing pursuits than hanging around Levitation Latte.

Oh, well. I supposed I'd hear what was going
on with Tom's funeral through the grapevine
sooner or later.

Because my house was more or less on the way to
Max's place, Deanne and Mike picked me up so we
wouldn't have to take separate cars. There was
actually plenty of room to park up to four or five
vehicles in front of his oversized garage, but I
hadn't bothered to argue the point. I was feeling
just edgy enough at the thought of having to
conduct a séance that I was all too happy to let
someone else take the wheel.

Al was manning the gate to the ranch as we
drove up and immediately waved us in, even
though he shouldn't have recognized Deanne's
RAV4, which was better suited to hauling around
four people than Mike's truck. Then again, I'd sent
Max another text late in the afternoon after we'd
set up our carpool plans, and so he'd probably let

Al know to be on the lookout for a car that wasn't my dusty old Subaru.

We all got out of the SUV, Deanne's eyes widening a bit as she surveyed her surroundings. We'd arrived at Sunset Ridge at the time of day that had given the ranch its name, and warm orange light from the setting sun bathed the hilltop and painted the leaves in shades of amber and gold.

"Wow," she said. "I knew the view here would be incredible, but...."

"It is pretty spectacular," I agreed. "And awesome in the summer when you can sit out on the patio."

Not that we'd be dining *al fresco* tonight, I was sure. The days were still nice and mild, in the upper sixties or just touching seventy degrees, but as soon as the sun went down, it got cold pretty darn fast.

The three of us made our way over to the entry under its pretty little portico, and Mike rang the bell. A moment later, Max opened the door and smiled at us, looking spectacular himself in a dark gray suit with a deep steel-blue dress shirt underneath. No tie, though; apparently he'd decided the spirits would be okay with him dressing down just a little.

Not that someone could probably be viewed as "dressing down" when they were wearing a five-thousand-dollar suit.

"Hey," he said. "Come on in."

We stepped into the foyer and exchanged greetings. The whole time, though, I couldn't ignore the way his gaze kept traveling toward me, or how his eyes had widened in surprise when he'd first caught sight of me in my purple dress.

Maybe I needed to listen to Deanne more often.

And since I caught a glimpse of just the faintest smirk playing at the corner of her mouth as we all followed Max into the dining room, I guessed she'd noticed his reaction, too. Mike, as seemed to be the case with most guys, appeared to be blissfully oblivious to those undercurrents, however.

Delicious smells were coming out of the kitchen, and I breathed in deeply as we took our various seats around the gorgeous live-edge dining room table, which looked as though it had been cut from a single trunk of an enormous tree, maybe a redwood. After settling my napkin in my lap, I said, "I still can't believe you made Lou cook for all of us."

"Nah, he loves it," Max replied, then added in response to Mike's mystified look, "Lou's one of my bodyguards. But his Sicilian grandmother taught him how to cook, and who am I to say no to that?"

"I think it's awesome," Deanne said. "And it smells great."

"I think you'll find it's better than any pizza

you can get in town," Max said, and shot me a grin. "Well, except maybe yours, Skye."

"He probably has me beat," I replied, not offended in the slightest. "I didn't have a Sicilian grandmother to teach me, after all."

Even as I uttered those words, however, I couldn't quite ignore the pang that went through me. I knew my mother was Italian, but I didn't know whether she'd been Sicilian or not. Maybe I really did have a grandmother like Lou's out there somewhere, someone who could've taught me the finer points of pizza-making.

Max didn't quite wink at me, but I could tell he was glad I hadn't been upset by his praise of Lou's pizza. Reaching for the oversized straw-wrapped bottle that had been sitting near his place at the head of the table, he said, "And I hope you're all okay with chianti."

Deanne and Mike made murmurs of assent, while I said, "Where in the world did you get that wine?"

Because I knew for damn sure that neither the Lowe's grocery store or our local Walmart carried anything like that.

Mouth quirking, Max said, "Oh, I made another trip into Santa Fe today and went to the Total Wine there. I wanted to get something fun for dinner tonight."

Deanne's brows lifted ever so slightly. "You

went all the way to Santa Fe just to get a bottle of wine?"

Without missing a beat, Max replied, "Well, I might have picked up a *little* more than just one bottle."

Everyone chuckled at that remark, and then we were quiet as he got up from his seat and walked around the table, filling our wine glasses from the enormous bottle of chianti. Even though there were four of us, I somehow doubted we'd be able to finish the whole thing.

And for all I knew, maybe I shouldn't have been drinking even the slightest bit. Maybe alcohol would interfere with communing with the spirits, or whatever.

But Max had already filled my glass, so I decided to roll with it. I could always stop after this one drink if I decided that was the wise thing to do.

As soon as Max returned to his seat, Lou came in, wearing a floury apron and carrying a gorgeous pizza pie topped with pepperoni and sausage and olives and green peppers. In one of my earlier texts, I'd assured Max that none of us had any dietary limitations, and so it seemed he'd passed the word along to his bodyguard/chef to do what he liked.

"Thanks, Lou," I said as he deposited the pie on the table between Max and me. "This looks incredible."

"I've got another one prepped and ready to go

in case you need more," he replied. "*Buon appetito!*"

And with that, he headed back into the kitchen.

Once again, Max was the gracious host, dishing up generous slices for each of us before returning to his seat. "Lou is a happy clam," he told us. "I got him one of those pizza ovens that cooks in something like three minutes or whatever, so he's been having a lot of fun playing with it."

I could imagine. Not too long ago, I'd actually investigated getting one of those for myself, since I did enjoy making pizza from time to time, and the limitations of a regular oven made themselves pretty clear when you were attempting to get that genuine fire-baked char on your crust. However, a little research soon told me I couldn't really justify the cost, and so I'd abandoned the idea.

Obviously, Max didn't need to worry about the price of a pizza oven, however.

One bite told me maybe I needed to revisit my decision not to buy one. If I saved up for a couple of months....

"This is amazing," Deanne said after a moment of reverent silence. "Did you know Lou could cook like this when you hired him?"

"Nope," Max said cheerfully. "Just an extra little happy dividend." He set down his own slice and then reached for his glass of chianti. "I think we should all drink to a successful séance."

Oh, right. I'd been so overwhelmed by the flavors of that amazing pizza pie, I'd almost managed to forget the real reason why we were all here. Fighting the little flutter of unease that moved through my stomach, I picked up my own glass and waited while Deanne and Mike got theirs.

We all made dutiful little clinks and then drank, murmuring various comments like "to our séance." Once we were done, an awkward silence fell.

Wanting to fill it—and also wanting to discuss something other than my upcoming convo with the dead—I turned toward Mike and said, "Do you know anyone who's going to run in the special election?"

I'd caught him mid-bite, and so he had to swallow hastily before he replied, "No. I mean, obviously Alex Donnelly is running, but no one around City Hall has made any noises about trying to run against him."

"Special election?" Max inquired.

Right—I somehow doubted he was on the city government's email list, and he'd spent half the day running to Santa Fe and back, and therefore probably hadn't set foot anyplace where he'd see one of Cory Sills' little blue flyers. I explained what was going on, adding, "It might turn out that Alex runs uncontested, but they still have to have their meeting tomorrow just so everything's kosher."

Max's expression turned thoughtful. "Maybe I should run."

I couldn't help it—I let out a peal of startled laughter before I recovered myself. "You?"

"Why not?" he said, his tone somewhat wounded. Clearly, he hadn't appreciated my reaction to his comment. "It's not like I don't have the free time."

"Right now," I pointed out. "Aren't you jetting off to Costa Rica in January for your next shoot?"

He looked almost startled, as if he'd forgotten about his upcoming gig, even as Mike said, "That's an interesting idea, Max, but I don't think you've established permanent residency here, have you?"

Now he sent us all a wry smile. "Well, no. Although I've been thinking about it—New Mexico state income tax is a heck of a lot lower than it is in California."

I hadn't even thought of that. To my mind, there were even greater inducements to living in New Mexico permanently than saving some money on income tax, but if that's what it took....

"Well, maybe the next election," Deanne put in with a grin, and Max only shook his head.

"Maybe."

After that, the conversation moved to the fancy new pizza oven he'd bought, the speculation that

Las Vegas might actually be getting a second grocery store, and some back-and-forth about whether the upcoming winter was going to be a mild or a wet one.

Anything to avoid talking about Tom Gallegos and his murder, as if we all somehow knew we needed to hold those thoughts in reserve until the time for the séance actually rolled around.

Which it did about an hour later, after we'd eaten our fill of gourmet pizza and made a serious dent in the huge bottle of chianti Max had bought. I hadn't quite been able to stick to one glass, but on the second round, I'd told him to stop before my wine glass was even half full, and I hoped that bit of moderation would be enough to ensure psychic success.

We cleared the table and replaced our glasses of wine with water. No sign of Lou; the kitchen had been tidied up but was otherwise empty, telling me he'd taken off once his chef duties were complete.

Just as well. I was keyed up enough about conducting a séance without having one of Max's bodyguards as a witness.

With the table empty and awaiting our convo with the spirits, we all resumed our seats. I drank some water, and Max sent me an expectant look. "So...what should we all do?"

Good question. The only séances I'd ever seen had been fake ones on TV, and although I'd tried to do little research on my phone that afternoon in between customers, I couldn't exactly call myself an expert.

Bumbling amateur, more like it.

We really should have cleansed the space with something like palo santo wood, but that sort of thing was in short supply in Las Vegas. I'd settled for swiping a salt shaker after I'd dropped my plate off in the kitchen, figuring if I did contact something I couldn't quite handle, a healthy sprinkling of salt should be enough to banish the evil entity.

At least, that was what I'd read. Another article had advised me it was generally bad juju to reach out to the soul of someone who was recently dead, but since that was the whole reason for why we'd gathered here at Max's place, I'd decided to ignore that bit of folk wisdom.

One thing we'd done right was to attempt the ritual in a friendly, welcoming place. While a lot of people thought a séance should be conducted in a creepy old house or a graveyard or whatever, it was a lot smarter to do this sort of thing in a location that offered mental and spiritual support. Maybe it would have been even smarter to have congregated at my house instead of Max's, but I hadn't known the location would be such an important factor when I accepted his invitation, and now I just needed to roll with it.

I drew in a breath and did my best to answer

his question honestly. "Mostly, you just need to be still and quiet, and focus as best you can on the person you're attempting to contact. Good thoughts, though—don't think about how Tom was killed. Just concentrate on who he was when he was alive and how we would like him to tell us anything he needs to communicate."

And hope like hell that the one thing he really wanted to get across to the land of the living was exactly who'd sent him to the afterlife. I couldn't ask the question point-blank because I needed to do the best I could to send out waves of friendly, empathetic energy.

One thing I had asked Max for was some white candles. A group of three pillars sat on a black iron tray at the center of the table, although they'd stayed unlit during dinner.

"Could you light the candles now?" I asked, and he nodded, rising from his chair so he could fetch an Aim-N-Flame from the sideboard behind us.

With that matter settled, it was time to get to business.

My heart was beating faster than I would have liked, and I prayed the nerves would go away as I settled into the ritual. "Breathe deeply," I said, doing my best to keep my voice soft and soothing, like someone giving a guided meditation. I'd never done that, either, but at least I'd listened to a few and so knew a little more about what one should sound like. "Do your best to let your thoughts focus only on Tom Gallegos, on the good things you remember about him."

No one responded to me directly, but they all closed their eyes in response to my request—even Mike, who'd been looking uncomfortable but at least hadn't voiced any objections.

I followed suit, eyes shut and thoughts doing their best to concentrate on Tom, remembering how he'd looked, the sound of his voice, the way he'd walked.

The way he always had a ready smile for everyone, no matter how busy he might have been.

With all those details fixed in my mind, I figured it was time to try reaching out.

"Tom," I said softly. "It's Skye O'Malley, and Deanne and Mike Daniels, and Max Sullivan. We'd like to speak with you. Is there something you'd like to tell us?"

Absolutely nothing. The silence in the room was so heavy, I found myself wishing I'd had Max put on some calm music in the background, something to break up the way I thought I could hear my own pulse thudding in my eardrums. But it was too late for that, and so I knew I had to soldier ahead.

Well, all the articles I'd read had told me it

often took a while to make contact. I just had to keep trying.

Easier said than done, though. I might have exhorted my friends not to think about the unfortunate circumstances of Tom's demise, but the more I tried to put them out of my head, the more those gruesome thoughts swirled around in my brain, dead leaves floating on a cold graveyard wind.

Enough of that. Another article had suggested a visualization of myself surrounded by white light, of connecting with the spirit inside me so that the spirit I was attempting to contact would see me as one of his own, rather than something alien trying to force a connection.

Okay, white light. I breathed in again and summoned an image of white light enveloping me, sort of like a toga made of luminous stardust. That glowing self seemed to float in a glade of fresh grass, surrounded by the slender shapes of willow trees. Nothing anywhere around Las Vegas looked remotely like the scene I was imagining, but it was pretty...with any luck, pretty enough to attract Tom Gallegos' spirit.

At least, that's what I was hoping.

"Tom," I said aloud. "We mean you no harm. We only want to hear the truth from your lips."

And...still nothing.

I released a small breath, not loud enough to be

a sigh—and hopefully not loud enough for anyone else seated at the table to have heard. This wasn't the time for impatience, but I couldn't quite stop myself from wondering exactly how long I would have to sit here, imagining myself in an idyllic scene that would be enticing enough to attract Tom Gallegos' spirit.

But then I saw movement in the distance and between the trees, as though someone was walking toward me through the shimmering spring-green glade I'd concocted as my otherworldly meeting place. My heart sped up for a moment...until I realized that wasn't Tom approaching, but a woman.

For a few moments, I stared at her, struck by her air of familiarity, even though I didn't think I'd ever seen her before. When she got closer, though, she smiled...and realization struck with the power of a lightning bolt.

The woman was my grandmother Maureen.

I hadn't recognized her at first because the woman I looked at now was only someone I'd seen in photos from the seventies or maybe early eighties, her hair its original fawn brown and without the lines and sags of age blurring her features. But her bright blue eyes were the same, even though they looked at me now with something that seemed a little too close to disappointment for my taste.

"G-Grandma?" I managed, and her smile returned.

"Yes, Skye."

"You look different."

The dimple at one corner of her mouth—a dimple I wished I'd inherited, but no luck—made a brief appearance. "We can choose how we want to appear on this plane," she told me. "I liked myself at this age, so this is the way I present myself."

I could see that—she looked as though she was probably a few years older than I, so in her early thirties somewhere. A woman in the full of life, beautiful and happy. This would have been before my grandfather died way too young, and when my father and my uncle were just little boys.

This woman probably thought she had absolutely everything going for her.

"Well, you look great." I stopped there and glanced past her, but we were alone here.

No sign of Tom Gallegos.

My grandmother must have guessed what I was doing, because she said, "Oh, he isn't coming. A spirit who's arrived on this plane so recently isn't anyone you should be trying to contact in this way."

Something the articles had tried to tell me, but I'd been too stubborn to heed their advice. Still, all wasn't lost, since Grandma Maureen was here.

"Well, can you tell me who killed him?" I asked next, figuring that if she was a spirit, then she must be privy to everything that was happening on Earth as well.

Her mouth pursed. "That's not my story to tell. And Skye, you really shouldn't be attempting to contact this plane in this way. This sort of thing isn't where your talents—even though they've turned out to be quite astonishing—lie."

Ever since Max had brought up the topic of holding a séance, I'd wondered if I was getting myself into something a bit beyond me. My grandmother's words only seemed to prove those worries hadn't been unfounded.

Still, since she was here and talking to me, I wasn't quite ready to give up. "Then what am I supposed to do?"

"The universe communicates with you in its own way," she told me. "You should trust those talents and work with them, rather trying to force your gifts to do things they were never designed for."

"Like making a cat talk?" I asked, and now she grinned, her blue eyes crinkling with amusement.

"No, that's different," she replied. "That kind of magic is confined to your plane, instead of reaching out to this one." A pause, and she added, "However that particular spell works out in the end, it's between you and the cat. Remember to trust your intuition, and don't try to force it." A pause, and then she laid a hand on my arm, a reassuring touch even though she wasn't corporeal and therefore I couldn't really feel anything. "I'm so proud of what you're becoming. Best of luck, my dear."

"But—" I began, and stopped myself. Even as the word had started to emerge from my lips, she grew hazy and transparent before she disappeared entirely, leaving me alone in the glade.

Trust my intuition. Let my talents work the way they were supposed to.

I didn't quite know what I was supposed to do with that advice—although I felt a happy little glow inside at my grandmother's praise—but I did know one thing.

This would be the last séance I ever held.

CHAPTER 11

Public Service

I opened my eyes to see Max and Deanne and Mike all watching me expectantly. Naturally, Max was the first to speak.

"Well?" he said, blue eyes focused with laser intensity on my face.

An unwelcome blush touched my cheeks in response to that too-bright stare, but I told myself he wouldn't be able to detect my embarrassing flush in the dim, candlelit room. "I made contact," I said, then hurried on before any of my companions could get too excited, "but it was with my grandmother, not Tom Gallegos. She told me he was too recently dead for me to communicate with him, and that I needed to find out who his murderer was some other way."

Deanne blinked. "Why would she say that?"

"Because I guess it's a thing," I replied, still irritated with myself for attempting a séance in the first place when all the signs had been telling me it was a very bad idea. "Newly dead spirits need time to settle into their new existence and not get dragged back to the plane they just left. Or something like that."

Neither Max nor Deanne looked too thrilled by my explanation, while Mike just appeared impassive, as though he was putting up with all this for Deanne's sake and didn't believe a word of it.

Okay, that wasn't entirely fair. He knew my tea leaf reading was the real deal, because it was the leaves that told him the perfect job was coming up for him with the city and that he shouldn't expand his employment search to Santa Fe, which was what he'd been about to do at the time. Sure enough, the position with the community development office appeared on the city's website the very next day.

And sure, some people might have tried to say I'd been tipped off by one of my customers, someone who worked for the city's HR department, but that wasn't what had happened at all. Mike had believed me—and was thrilled that he wouldn't have to face an hour commute each way to get a decent-paying job—and that was the important thing.

"Well, so now what?" Max said, his brows drawing together in frustration.

"We do what my grandmother told me to do," I replied. While I could sympathize with his feeling of getting stymied at every turn, there wasn't much we could do about it at the moment. "She seems to think that my normal means of getting messages from other planes should be enough."

"But you read some tea leaves and didn't come up with anything," Deanne pointed out, and I shrugged.

"I know," I told her. "And it's been bugging me ever since that I couldn't make sense of the reading. But that doesn't mean the clues weren't good ones. It just means I haven't been able to put them together yet."

Looking dejected, she slumped against her seat, while Max drummed his fingers on the tabletop.

"You saw a shovel and a cloverleaf, right?"

I nodded. "Both supposedly good luck symbols, which doesn't make any sense when you're talking about a murder. But again, there could be some kind of connection that I'm just not seeing right now."

He released a breath and looked as though he was about to say something else, then gave a very small shake of his head. Most likely, he'd realized there wasn't any point in tearing apart those two very minor clues, since I'd been pondering them for days and hadn't come up with a single theory that made any sense.

Mike seemed to take this break in the conversation as a signal that it was time to call it quits for now, because he said, "Well, it doesn't look as if we're going to get anything new tonight, and you and Deanne both have to be up early for work. I think it's time to head out."

As much as I would have liked to argue with him, I knew he was right. No amount of chewing over the problem was going to induce a burst of inspiration. Much better to go home and get a decent night's sleep, and try to look at the situation with fresh eyes in the morning.

Deanne seemed to realize the same thing, because she heaved a sigh and said, "You're right, honey—it's a work night." Her gaze moved to Max as she added, "Thanks so much for playing host. The pizza was fab."

He smiled, although something about his expression looked a little forced. I got the feeling he would have liked to try coaxing us to stay a while longer but realized he was outvoted.

"I'll send your compliments to the chef," he said, and rose from his chair.

The rest of us got up as well, and were a pretty silent bunch as we headed toward the door, Max trailing behind. Just as Mike was heading outside, Max laid a hand on my arm.

"Thank you," he said in a murmur. "I know you tried."

"I wish I could've done more," I told him. "But I'm not giving up."

The smile he sent me now looked much more genuine than the one he'd put on a few minutes earlier. "Oh, I know you're not. And neither am I."

I inclined my head just the slightest bit and then was out the door. Maybe the evening hadn't gone exactly as planned, but Max had reached out and touched me, had put his hand on my arm as though doing such a thing was entirely natural.

That had to count for something...even if I wasn't entirely sure what.

None of us said much on the drive back to town. As Mike pulled into my driveway, I said, "Thanks for being the chauffeur."

He shrugged. "No problem. I'm glad I could do something to help."

"You do a lot," Deanne told him, then shifted in her seat so she could look over her shoulder at me. "See you in the morning."

"See you," I echoed, and undid my seatbelt so I could climb out of the back seat and head up the front walk to the porch.

They waited in the driveway until I was safely inside, and then I heard the RAV4 back out and drive away slowly.

After seeing her on that other plane, I felt my grandmother's presence in the house more strongly than ever, despite all the remodeling I'd had done recently. I stood in the middle of the living room and said in a tentative voice, "Grandma?"

Only silence met my ears. She might have come to talk to me in that other world, but it seemed as though she had no intention of visiting this one.

Probably just as well. I had enough on my plate as it was.

I walked over to the stairs, flipped the switch to turn off the living room light and turn on the one to illuminate the staircase, then made my way up the steps.

Time to go to bed.

The next morning, I was mixing the batter for a batch of pumpkin chocolate chunk muffins when it suddenly hit me.

I needed to go the meeting tonight, the one where anyone who wanted to run for the open mayor's seat was supposed to announce their intentions and get on the ballot.

Where that notion had come from, I had absolutely no idea. Honestly, I hadn't been planning to attend the meeting, since I figured I'd hear the play-by-play from Deanne, who always went to anything city-related as a show of support for her husband. She probably wanted to make sure she seemed like a real team player, since

Mike's boss was only a few years from retirement and she was hoping Mike would get bumped to the head of the line when Bob Lopez stepped down from the position he'd held for more than fifteen years.

"Can I come with you tonight?" I asked her as soon as she came into the kitchen. By that point, I'd already fed Tilly, who'd promptly escaped out the cat door as soon as she'd inhaled a bowl of Salmon Surprise.

Deanne blinked at me. "Come with me where?"

"To the meeting," I replied.

Her confused expression only deepened. "You never go to stuff like that."

"I do sometimes," I told her.

She pulled an apron off its hook and tied it around her waist, and then yanked the mini-scrunchie from her wrist so she could pull back her long blonde hair. "Only if it's zoning or something that affects the downtown business district."

Well, that was true enough. Bridge Street and its immediate environs had been designated as a special district so the businesses there could have access to special grants and other types of funding designed to help us maintain the century-old buildings. There were also other parts of town that had been designated as historic neighborhoods, making it so the homeowners there couldn't just tear down their lovely old houses and put up condos or something.

Not that there was much call for condos in Las Vegas, New Mexico.

"Okay," I allowed. "But something's telling me I need to go to the meeting tonight."

At once, Deanne's smoky-blue eyes lit up. "Ooh, a clue?"

"Maybe," I said. "I don't know for sure. It's not like my grandmother's ghost popped in to tell me I had to go because I'd hear something that would help solve Tom Gallegos' murder. It's just a feeling. A twinge, I guess."

That explanation seemed to be enough to convince my friend, because she looked positively giddy. "It's your intuition," she informed me in tones of supreme confidence. "Just like your grandmother told you when you talked to her last night. She said you needed to trust your intuition, and now it's already sending you signals."

I wasn't sure it exactly worked that way, but I wasn't going to argue with her. Something seemed to be nudging me in the direction of the meeting, and I knew I'd be stupid to ignore that odd inner tingling, or whatever you wanted to call it.

Maybe I'd be bored to tears, but wild horses couldn't keep me away from that particular town hall.

As our work day came to a close, Deanne offered to drive me to the meeting, but I demurred.

"It's fine," I told her. "But I can meet you and Mike there."

She looked vaguely disappointed—maybe she'd been hoping the three of us could go out for drinks or something after the town hall ended—but she didn't argue. "Okay," she said as she shouldered her purse and we both headed toward the back door of the shop. "Meet you there."

"Definitely."

Tilly had already been taken care of...and had offered the disappointing news that she hadn't seen anything of interest that afternoon, unless you wanted to count the load of fish Arnie Martinez had dropped into the dumpster behind his restaurant earlier that day.

"But it had already turned," the cat said sadly. "So I didn't touch any of it."

"Good call," I told her, even as I did my best to ignore my disappointment at the complete lack of any actionable intelligence from my feline charge.

Some spy she was turning out to be.

I'd gone back and forth on whether I should ask Max if he wanted to come to the meeting, and finally had decided against it. All day had been radio silence from him, and I wasn't sure what to do about that. Had he decided he'd gone a little too far by reaching out to touch my arm the night before, or was he annoyed by my complete failure as a medium?

Honestly, I had to hope there was some other reason as to why I hadn't heard from him, but I decided it was better to leave sleeping dogs lie.

Besides, having Max attend the meeting would certainly fuel speculation that he was planning on running—even though, strictly speaking, he wasn't eligible—and that would pull focus from any real candidates who decided to throw their hats in the ring. If he'd reached out and asked if I was attending, and then suggested he wanted to tag along, that would have been one thing.

But he hadn't, and that seemed to be the end of the matter.

I went home and changed out of my work clothes and into a nicer shirt and jeans, then had some soup and salad for dinner. Only a glass of water, though, and no wine, since I would be heading back out in just a little bit.

Obviously, way more people were interested in attending this particular meeting than was usual for these types of gatherings, because the parking lot at City Hall was full and I had to park my Subaru almost a block away. As I was making my way to the entrance, my path crossed that of someone I certainly hadn't been expecting to see.

Max.

He waved and quickened his pace when we made eye contact. As he fell into step beside me, he said, "I didn't think you'd be coming tonight."

Because Max was a master of the unexpected, I couldn't let his presence here rattle me too much. Adopting an airy tone, I replied, "Oh, I decided I should check it out. I got a funny little tingle that said I needed to be here."

Like Deanne, he almost lit up at that news. "So, maybe your grandmother was right about trusting your instincts."

"Maybe," I said. "I guess we'll just have to see if there are any interesting developments or whether this meeting is going to be the same old, same old."

His mouth twitched. "Yeah, I guess we'll just have to see."

A definite murmur went through the crowd as the two of us entered the auditorium, now almost filled to capacity. I spotted Mike and Deanne off to the side in the second-to-last row, an empty seat next to them, one they'd obviously been saving for me.

Well, darn.

Max followed my gaze, then leaned down and said in a low voice, "You can go ahead and sit with them. I should have told you I was coming."

True, but I would much rather sit next to him. Deanne would understand.

I hoped.

"No, it's okay," I said quickly. "Besides, there are a couple of empty seats right behind them in the last row. Let's run and get them before someone else sits there."

Luckily, he didn't argue, but only hurried toward the pair of seats I'd mentioned. We might have been out of luck, but Deanne, bless her, saw at once what we were doing and pulled off her cardigan and tossed it onto the chairs in question, thereby saving them from Lucy Margolis and her husband Martin, who apparently had also seen the empty seats and were beginning to head in that direction.

I would have felt bad about cutting my neighbors off at the pass, except there were still a few seats at the end of the row, and it was easy enough for the couple to course-correct and sit in those ones instead.

"Thanks," I said, sounding breathless as I lifted Deanne's sweater from my chair and sat down.

"Not a problem," she replied with a grin, and took the cardigan from me so she could drape it over her lap. Looking over at Max, she said, "If we'd known you were coming, we would've saved you a seat, too."

"It's fine," he said, and seated himself as well. Those folding chairs weren't exactly the most comfortable or generous things in the world, and so his leg almost brushed against mine as he leaned forward to talk to Deanne.

Almost.

Well, I'd just have to figure out a way to have my leg touch his sometime before the evening was over.

Purely by accident, of course.

"It was sort of a last-minute decision," he went on. "I never attended anything like this when I lived here before, but now that I'm back, I figure it couldn't hurt to get a little more involved with the community."

Possibly gearing up for a future run at the mayor's seat? I definitely didn't want to ask that question in such a public place. For all I knew, he was mostly doing his best to be out and about in order to make a Max Sullivan sighting just another aspect of living in Las Vegas, and certainly nothing of any note.

Judging by the reaction to him sitting with all us peons, it looked like it was going to take a while for our hometown to achieve that level of nonchalance. People kept whispering to one another and shooting not-so-surreptitious glances in Max's and my direction, although...to my huge relief...no one seemed inclined to approach him directly. Maybe they'd decided that a meeting to determine the next mayor after the first one had died under suspicious circumstances wasn't the best time to ask for an autograph.

The lights flickered, apparently a signal that we were about to get down to business, and the crowd quieted. Deanne, who'd been looking as though she wanted to respond to Max's comment, turned back around in her seat while wearing a resigned air, as if she knew she had to at least pretend to be interested in the proceedings.

Cory Sills walked out to a lectern that had been set up on the raised platform—too low to be called a stage—at the front of the auditorium. Even from where I sat, she looked strained and pale, but that seemed about par for the course. She already had a ton on her plate, and lots of people had issues with public speaking. God knows I wouldn't have wanted to be the one standing up there with what felt like the whole town's eyes on me.

"Good evening, everyone," she said. "Thank you for coming out tonight. We can make this brief. If anyone wants to be added to the ballot for the special mayoral election being held next Tuesday, please come up to the lectern and introduce yourself, and say a few words about why you're running for the office. I'll take down your names and then ask you to stay afterward to sign some paperwork so we can make it all official. We can start with you, Mr. Donnelly."

As expected, the deputy mayor got up from

one of the seats in the front row and made his way to the lectern. Alex Donnelly was around forty-eight or forty-nine, of medium height and trim of build, with fair hair he kept cut short and eyes whose color I'd never been able to determine exactly, mostly because he wore glasses all the time. I knew he stayed in shape because he ran every morning and had never once bought a muffin at Levitation Latte. Every once in a great while he'd come in for coffee, and on even rarer occasions would get a nonfat cappuccino, but he definitely wasn't a regular.

"Hello, everyone," he said. He had a pleasant voice that matched his equally inoffensive appearance. "I'm Alex Donnelly, and I've been the deputy mayor of Las Vegas for almost seven years now. I have the necessary experience to take on the duties as mayor, and, because of my accounting background, you can be sure the city's funds will be handled with the utmost care."

Some scattered clapping followed that statement. True, fiscal responsibility wasn't the sexiest topic in the world, but still, it was nice to know the city would be in good hands with someone like him.

"Talk about your perfect accountant," Max said to me in an undertone. "He looks like he's straight out of Central Casting."

With some effort, I smothered a snicker. I really

couldn't argue with my friend's statement, considering I'd been thinking just about the same thing. I lifted my shoulders but didn't reply, partly because the elderly man seated to Max's right was shooting us both the evil eye. It looked as though he didn't give a darn about my companion's celebrity status and would be all too willing to give us a dressing-down if we didn't shut up.

It seemed Max picked up on the guy's vibe as well, because he subsided and settled himself against the back of his folding chair, although something close to a smirk continued to play around his lips.

Our little exchange had distracted me from the remainder of Alex Donnelly's presentation, so I missed whatever he'd said next. Now he just leaned slightly closer to the microphone and concluded with, "Thank you for your support."

A smattering of applause emerged from the audience as he returned to his seat. Probably not the most ringing of endorsements, but at least it was better than dead silence.

Cory returned to the lectern. "Thank you, Mr. Donnelly," she said formally. "Is there anyone else?"

An uneasy silence met her question, but no one got up. Was this going to turn out to be an uncontested election?

Then there was a stir to one side of the auditorium as a tall, dark-haired man stood up. He seemed vaguely familiar, and then I realized why.

The man who'd stood was Dave Gallegos, Tom's younger brother.

I knew him even less well than the late mayor, mostly because Dave lived on the outskirts of Las Vegas and didn't seem to come into the city's downtown area very often. About all I did know was that he owned a construction company and was unmarried, a little unusual for a resident in his late thirties, since ours tended to be a family kind of town.

Cory stared at him, now looking flustered. "Mr. Gallegos?"

"That's right," he replied. "Is it okay if I come up and speak my piece?"

"Of course," she said, obviously doing her best to regain her composure. "That's what this meeting is for."

He walked over to the dais and then approached the lectern, while Cory stepped out of the way. For someone who wanted to run for mayor, he didn't exactly look the part. The chambray shirt and faded jeans he was wearing could have been the same outfit he'd put on to go to work that morning, and he looked tired, stubble covering his chin and with shadows under his dark eyes.

Well, of course he looks tired, I told myself. *He lost his brother just a couple of days ago.*

And unlike most people interested in public office, Dave Gallegos definitely appeared ill at ease in front of a crowd. A pause as he pushed a lock of dark hair off his forehead, and then he gripped the edges of the lectern and leaned toward the microphone.

"Hi," he said, and stopped again, as though he hadn't thought far enough ahead to really figure out what he intended to say. "I'm Dave Gallegos, and Tom Gallegos was my big brother. Anyone who knows me knows I'm not really the kind of person to do something like this, but...."

The words trailed off, and a sympathetic murmur went through the crowd as Dave Gallegos stood there, obviously wrestling with himself in an attempt to determine the best thing to say.

When he resumed his speech, his voice sounded stronger, a little more certain. Either inspiration had struck, or he'd at least found an inner reserve of courage that would allow him to go on.

"My brother had a lot of plans for this town, ideas that would make everyone's lives better," he said. "You know Tom was always thinking about what he could do for Las Vegas, and I know that's why you elected him for a second term. He won't be here"—Dave's voice cracked slightly, but he forced himself to continue—"he won't be here to see those plans realized, but I know I'll do my best to carry out his vision. And that's why you should vote for me."

The last sentence had barely escaped his lips before the crowd erupted into thunderous applause. He sort of nodded at everyone and then all but fled the stage so he could seek the refuge of the chair where he'd been sitting before he went up to the lectern.

Everyone kept clapping, though, until Cory came back to the microphone and cleared her throat. "Um...thanks for that, Dave," she said. Her voice sounded a little shaky, as though she'd also been affected by his speech. She looked into the crowd, adding, "Anyone else want to come up here?"

An immediate silence fell after she asked that question, which didn't surprise me too much. Dave Gallegos would be a tough act to follow. Even if a couple more people might have been considering whether or not to enter the race, it seemed clear they'd abandoned the idea as soon as the dead mayor's brother had decided to run for the empty seat.

"Okay, then," Cory said, her tone now much brisker. "The special election to fill the mayor's seat will be held on Tuesday, October twenty-fifth. Ballots will start going out tomorrow, so make sure to keep an eye out for those. Thank you all very much for coming tonight."

She stepped away from the microphone, and immediately, people in the audience started chattering, obviously wanting to start their discussions about Dave Gallegos' unexpected entry into the race right away.

Deanne shifted in her seat so she could eyeball Max and me. "So, what do you think about that?"

"I guess it makes sense," I replied. "I mean, it sounds like Tom talked to his brother a lot about what he wanted to do for the city, so Dave seems the logical person to carry on his work."

Mike, however, was frowning. "Dave doesn't have a single second of public service experience," he pointed out, and next to me, Max shrugged.

"You've gotta start somewhere, right?"

"True," Mike allowed. "But Tom was on the city council for two terms before he ran for mayor. He knows how city government works. Dave won't have a clue."

That sounded kind of harsh to me, but on the other hand, I could see where Mike was coming from. He'd been working for the city for years, and he probably knew all too well what it was like to have someone come in who didn't know the first thing about how small-town government worked.

Unfortunately for him—if the audience response was any indication—Dave sounded like a shoo-in for our next mayor.

"Well, we'll just have to see what happens," Deanne put in, her tone now slightly soothing.

Her husband shrugged. "I suppose so."

Since everyone else had started to filter out of the auditorium, we got up from our chairs as well and headed for the doors. As we were walking, Max's phone rang from inside his jacket pocket, and he took it out, brows pulling together slightly as he studied the message on the screen.

"Everything okay?" I asked in an undertone, and he nodded.

"Oh, sure."

But I noticed how he seemed preoccupied as we said goodbye to Deanne and Mike, and how he followed me as I began to walk toward my car. Not that I minded, but he definitely gave every indication of someone with a lot on their mind.

"Want to go get something to drink?" he asked abruptly as we approached my Subaru.

I turned toward him, startled. It had always been a fond dream of mine to have him ask me out for a drink, but I definitely hadn't been expecting that sort of invitation tonight.

"Um...sure," I replied, doing some quick mental math. The meeting had been very short, barely a half hour, and so it wasn't even eight o'clock yet. Plenty of time to go out for a drink...or two.

Something about his posture seemed to relax slightly. "Great. Bar Castañeda all right?"

"Sounds great." The bar at the historic hotel was definitely a better choice of venue than some of the dive-ier places around town.

"Meet you there, then."

He gave me a wave and headed off down the street. I couldn't see his Bronco, but I guessed he'd had to park even farther away from City Hall than I had.

No worries, though. Soon enough we'd have a table at the Bar Castañeda and then...

...well, and then I'd just have to see what happened.

CHAPTER 12

Far, Far Away

Even though he'd had to walk farther to get his car, somehow Max made it to the bar before I did. After I passed through the lobby and waved at the red-haired girl behind the counter—her name was Taylor Sweeney, and I'd babysat her back in junior high—I headed into the bar.

Or rather, the restaurant itself, since Max had gotten himself a table in one corner rather than back at the bar, which honestly didn't offer a lot of privacy. On that Wednesday night, there were plenty of tables available, so I supposed the management wouldn't mind too much if we used one of them solely for getting drinks and nothing else.

He smiled at me as I seated myself at the table. It seemed whatever had been contained in the text message he'd received as we walked out of the auditorium at City Hall, he'd had time to regain his composure.

"Thanks for humoring me," he said, and I allowed myself a small lift of my shoulders.

"Oh, it's fine," I replied, then added, "I mean, you're not keeping me up past my bedtime."

His eyes crinkled. "Good to know."

A server came over—a man a few years younger than either one of us, someone I didn't recognize—and Max and I both ordered a glass of tempranillo. The house wine was cheaper, of course, but I sort of doubted my movie star friend would miss that extra five bucks or so.

"So," I said, after the waiter had fetched our glasses of wine and we were left alone, "what's up? You seemed preoccupied back there."

"I was," Max admitted, and lifted his glass. "But it's all good. Problem is, I need to go to L.A. for a few days, and I probably won't be back until Sunday. I'm going to miss your birthday."

To be perfectly honest, I was kind of surprised that he'd even remembered my birthday was coming up on Friday. Besides, it wasn't as though I'd planned to make a big deal of it this year. Twenty-nine was an odd number anyway...not thirty yet, but still hovering at the edge of leaving that happy decade behind.

For whatever reason, twenty-nine felt a whole heck of a lot older than twenty-eight.

"Oh, it's okay," I said quickly. "I mean, I wasn't really planning to do anything special. Deanne and I were going to have a girls' night out and maybe head over to Santa Fe on Saturday."

Max didn't look too comforted by my reassurances. "Yeah, but I wanted to surprise you with dinner or something, and now I won't even be here."

That he'd put even that much thought into those sorts of plans startled me. After all, he hadn't mentioned the special day at all, and I'd just assumed he'd completely forgotten when it even was.

At the same time, I told myself not to read too much into Max's supposed plans. It was the sort of thing any friend might have done for another, and not some kind of huge romantic gesture.

Still....

"Well, you can take me out on Sunday when you get back," I said lightly. "If it won't be too late."

"No, I don't think so," Max replied. Something about his manner now seemed a bit easier, as if he'd realized I wasn't as upset by his impending absence as he'd thought I might be. "That is, I called my assistant on the way over here and told her she needed to book me a Sunday morning flight out of LAX. I'll be back here by mid-afternoon."

"Then that should work just fine," I told him, and sipped some of my tempranillo. For the millionth time, I told myself not to read too much into any of this. Max Sullivan was the sort of expansive person who always did his best to take care of the people close to him, whether they were friends or family members or girlfriends.

Even ex-girlfriends, I thought then, recalling how he'd set up that trust fund for Raylene and her kids.

He nodded, and I found the courage to ask, "Why *do* you need to go back to L.A.?"

Now Max looked almost furtive. He glanced around the restaurant, but the only other occupied tables were on the other side of the room, so there wasn't any real chance that someone could overhear what we were saying.

"I'm sworn to secrecy," he said, and I grinned.

"Seriously? What could be so secret?"

Again, he sent one of those surreptitious glances around the room. "It's a part...a big one," he told me. "But it's also super hush-hush, so I can't tell you anything more than that."

"A Marvel movie?" I inquired, undeterred.

As mobile and expressive as his features could be, Max was also a master of the deadpan look when it suited his purposes. Now he appeared almost stony-faced as he reached for his glass of wine and allowed himself a swallow. "I can't say one way or another."

A-ha. Or maybe he just wanted me to think it was a Marvel movie. But what else could be masked in such secrecy?

I tilted an eyebrow at him. "A Star Wars property?"

Maybe one muscle next to his mouth twitched. "I can't say."

"You don't have to," I told him. "You just gave it all away."

"I did not."

Smiling now, I drank some of my own tempranillo. When I put the glass down, I noticed at once that his expression was now resigned.

"Okay, it *is* a Star Wars thing," Max said. "But I honestly can't tell you anything more than that. Well, except it's something my agent has been working on in the background for a while now. I just didn't think they were going to move on it until after the first of the year."

"Maybe they decided they needed to talk to you now since you're going to be in Costa Rica in January," I suggested, and he nodded.

"That's the vibe I got," he said. "So, I'm flying out tomorrow, and I have a meeting with the execs on Friday. I was going to head right back to New Mexico after that, but there actually is a lot of stuff I really need to handle in person—things at the house, some paperwork I need to go over with my assistant. That's why I won't be coming back until Sunday."

"And it's fine," I responded at once. "This is huge. I wouldn't expect you to blow all that off just because Friday is my birthday."

As I spoke, I realized I really wasn't just blowing sunshine his way. This sounded like a once-in-a-lifetime opportunity, and I wouldn't allow myself to be the person who derailed it.

No, I'd have a quiet work day at the shop, and then Deanne and I would go out for drinks or something. I'd never been the kind of person to make a huge fuss out of birthdays, anyway. My grandmother had been like that, but after she was gone, I really didn't see the point. Considering the way my mother had bailed out only a few weeks after I was born, I generally didn't see my natal day as something worthy of celebration.

"Thanks for understanding," Max said. Now his eyes twinkled a bit, and he added, "And don't go solving Tom Gallegos' murder while I'm gone."

"Fat chance," I scoffed. "Considering I have absolutely no usable leads and my supposed feline spy isn't helping at all, I don't think I need to worry about making anyone do the perp walk while you're gone."

Max tilted his head at me, his expression still amused. "Hey, you never know when inspiration will strike. Remember what your grandmother told you."

How could I forget? It wasn't exactly the sort of encounter that might easily slip my mind. All the same, I thought her confidence in me was woefully misplaced. Yes, I had a few special psychic gifts, but they hadn't been of much use lately.

Saying any of that to Max would have sounded way too "woe is me," though, so I only replied, "Maybe. But I'm not going to hold my breath."

He reached over and patted my hand. "Don't underestimate yourself, Skye. You can be a real force of nature when you get going."

Now I really wanted to protest. If anyone sitting at this table was a force of nature, that would be Max Sullivan, the golden boy, the guy who made everything look easy.

Not quiet, dark little Skye, the girl teachers tended to ignore and who was generally picked last for any kind of sports team. Most of that shunning could have been laid squarely in the laps of Raylene and her cabal, since I actually was pretty decent at softball and soccer, but whatever. All that was long in the past.

Still, I had to think Max was grossly overestimating my abilities.

I didn't argue with him, though, partly because I didn't want him to think I was fishing for compliments by acting too modest. No, I'd let him believe what he wanted...and reserve my own judgment.

All the same, I really did hope there wouldn't be any major developments while he was out of town.

The only thing I told Deanne the next day was that Max had to go back to L.A. on business, and to my relief, she didn't pry.

On the other hand, that didn't mean she let the subject go completely.

"But he asked you out for a drink," she said. "That has to mean something."

"All it meant was that he wanted to go someplace quiet where we could talk," I replied. "Let's not make it anything more than it is."

"But he remembered your birthday," she protested. "Don't tell me that's not significant."

Because I honestly wasn't sure how I should interpret his concern on that topic, I didn't know exactly how to respond. The oven saved me from having to reply, though, with the timer going off at just the right moment.

I pulled the batch of blueberry muffins out of the oven, doing my best to ignore Deanne's remark...and hoping she'd get the hint and wouldn't keep pushing.

Luckily, she knew me well, and must have guessed I wanted to drop it. Instead, she commented, "Where do you want to go out for drinks tomorrow night? The Plaza? Bar Castañeda? Or do you want to go slumming and go to Blackie's?"

In a way, that last suggestion was kind of attractive, mostly because I knew they'd have live music... also because I knew there wouldn't be any chance of bumping into Kyle, since his band had already played there earlier in the week.

"How about we grab a bite at The Skillet and then head over to Blackie's after that?" I suggested. It was probably a good idea to lay down a base of tacos or burgers before we started seriously drinking, and also, it felt like the kind of casual way I should be spending the last birthday in my twenties.

"It's a plan," she told me.

I had to say it felt good to have our plans settled...even as I hoped nothing would come along to disrupt them.

But nothing much of note happened that Thursday, except Cory stopped by with another set of flyers, this time advertising the special election and exhorting everyone to make sure to cast their ballot.

"Turnout for these sorts of things tends to be low," she said as she handed me one of the flyers. "But I still want to do as much as I can to get everyone involved."

"I'll post it in the window, no problem," I told her. "When are the ballots going out?"

"Tomorrow," she replied promptly. "We got a rush job at the printer's, so we're going to drop them at the post office sometime tomorrow morning."

That seemed awfully fast, but Cory Sills was nothing if not efficient. Besides, it wouldn't be a complicated ballot, just a single option with two names representing two very different men.

I almost asked Cory what she thought of the two candidates, then decided that wasn't a very good idea. She must have had her own opinion of the situation, but that didn't mean she would feel comfortable discussing an election where she had to do her best to sound completely neutral on the topic. Her job was secure, because she kept her position no matter who was elected as mayor, and yet I could totally understand why she might have her own preferences as to who would be her next boss.

"I'll keep an eye out for mine," I said, and she smiled at me and hurried off, clearly intent on distributing as many of the flyers before lunch as possible.

And Tilly sure wasn't being of much use. As soon as she'd come in that morning, I inquired as to whether she'd noticed anything interesting as she went about her nighttime perambulations, but once again she only gave a little cat shrug and told me the town had been particularly boring the night before, then buried her face in a bowl of Seafood Medley.

So much for that. I thought Max's belief that I might solve the murder while he was still in Los Angeles had about as much odds of happening as me winning the lottery.

And since I didn't even play the lottery, those were some pretty long odds.

Guilt at not doing enough haunted me all afternoon, and when I got home, I resolved to do another reading even though I had a sneaking suspicion it would be an utter waste of my time.

Which it was. Or rather, it showed me the same two things I'd seen during the first go-'round.

A clover. A shovel, or spade. This time they were positioned on the opposite side of the cup from where I'd first seen them, but that didn't mean much, as the leaves were still lodged firmly halfway up the side.

Ugh. This wasn't making any sense at all.

I rinsed out the cup and wiped it off, then put it back in the cupboard. Well, at least I'd tried, even if I didn't have anything to show for my efforts.

Even as I started putting together a salad for dinner, my thoughts kept picking at those two symbols. Why did they keep showing up? Why was I seeing good luck signs when Tom Gallegos had experienced the very worst luck of all by being murdered?

I hadn't seen Kyle that day, either, which I found somewhat annoying. Even though I had to keep up my guard around him lest he think I was interested in rekindling our relationship, he was still my best source of inside information when it came to any crimes that had been committed within the town's limits. Was he keeping away on purpose? Had I said something to offend him?

Even though I wracked my brains, I really couldn't come up with anything that might have put him off...unless he was annoyed that I hadn't attended his gig on Tuesday night.

No, that was silly. He knew how early I had to get up, and since the sets at Blackie's generally started just as I was going to bed, the likelihood of my attending had been pretty much zero.

And all right, Deanne and I were planning to

go there tomorrow night, but that was different. We didn't work Saturdays, and therefore could stay up as late on Friday night as we pleased.

I was definitely grumpier than I would have liked when I went to bed that night, but my foul mood didn't prevent me from sleeping soundly. Too soundly, really; it would have been nice if the universe had decided to lend me a hand and send me one of my true dreams, something that could have guided me toward the answers I was looking for, but if I dreamed that night, I couldn't remember a single one of them when I woke up.

Fine. Well, I'd have to do my best to let it all go. Max was headed out of town, and tea leaves and dreams were obviously getting me nowhere. I just needed to focus on enjoying my birthday and let the experts handle Tom Gallegos' murder.

Not that this morning felt too different from any other. The sun was still sleeping below the horizon as I drove to Levitation Latte, and the same chores were still waiting for me when I got there.

But I decided to make a batch of macadamia nut and white chocolate chip muffins because they were some of my favorites, and I got a pot of mocha java brewing in addition to the usual French or Italian roast. And when Deanne showed up about a half hour after I got in, she was carrying a festive metallic blue gift bag festooned with swirly ribbons.

"Happy birthday!" she exclaimed, and gave me a quick hug. Luckily, I'd just started setting out the ingredients for a batch of croissants and therefore hadn't been in the middle of something too complicated, and so I could return the hug with a smile.

"You didn't have to get me anything," I told her—the same thing I said to her every year when my birthday rolled around.

And, just like always, she sent me a deprecating look.

"Are you serious? Like I'm not going to go shopping for my best friend?"

True, shopping was one of Deanne's favorite pastimes, even if the pickings were kind of slim in our town. I brushed some stray flour off my hands and onto my apron, then took the gift bag from her.

Inside was a gorgeous cashmere sweater, wrap style and in a luscious dark teal color. "It's beautiful," I said as I lifted it out of the bag and held it up against me—carefully, so I wouldn't get any flour on the gorgeous knit.

"I thought you could wear it on a date with Max," she said slyly.

Right. I lowered the sweater back into its bag and replied, "Max and I don't go on 'dates.'"

"Yet," she said, her tone heavy with significance.

"Ever," I corrected her, and she narrowed her eyes at me.

"Oh, please," she returned. "What do you want to call what you did Wednesday night after the meeting at City Hall?"

"Drinks with a friend," I said firmly. "That's all. He wanted to apologize for not being here for my birthday."

Deanne sent me a look that could only be described as pitying, like she didn't want to think anyone could be so dense. "Yeah, and what kind of guy would make a gesture like that if he didn't want a little more?"

As much as I wanted to believe her, I knew she was barking up entirely the wrong tree—a tree that also happened to be located in the wrong forest. "That's just how Max is. If you're his friend, he takes care of you. There's absolutely nothing romantic about any of it."

Her expression told me she didn't believe my words of protest. However, even though we'd all gone to the same schools and had been around each other for literally decades, I flattered myself that I still knew Max Sullivan a lot better than she did. There hadn't been a single hint in his tone or expression or any of his actions to indicate he was being anything but friendly.

And okay, there had been that one flicker of admiration in his eyes when he'd seen me the night of the séance, but I could chalk that reaction up to fancy feathers and nothing more.

"But I love the sweater," I added quickly, in case she didn't think I was grateful for the present. "It'll be great for Christmas."

One eyebrow lifted, but to my relief, it didn't seem as though she planned to push any more buttons regarding Max and his feelings for me...or lack thereof. Instead, she went on in a very different tone, "Oh, and Mike offered to play chauffeur tonight so I don't have to worry about being the designated driver. He said it was his little birthday present for you."

I'd been about to protest that he didn't need to do that, but because Deanne had explained it was a present, I decided it was better to keep my mouth shut. Besides, I doubted we'd be out super late. We might not have to get up early the next morning, but today was a regular work day, and staying out past midnight when I'd been awake since four-thirty seemed like a recipe for disaster.

So I smiled at her and told her it was awesome of Mike to do that for us, and left it there. It seemed the two of them were determined to make sure I had the best birthday possible, even if Max wouldn't be here for it.

And so what? I asked myself as I returned to my

neglected croissant dough and Deanne headed out into the shop to make sure everything was tidy and ready for opening. *He hasn't been here for your birthday the past ten years, either. What makes this one different?*

Nothing, really. Except....

Except now he was back in my life. In exactly what capacity, I still hadn't figured out.

Maybe I never would.

CHAPTER 13

Out on the Town

T he day passed quickly, though, despite my getting into a bit of a heated discussion with Tilly when she reappeared a little before three o'clock.

"I am not coming to stay with you!" she snapped.

Luckily, Deanne was up front with a customer, and the door to the combo kitchen/storeroom at the rear of the shop was shut. Otherwise, I had no doubt our current patron would have wondered who the heck I was arguing with back there.

I put my hands on my hips. "Look, it was one thing to let you go roaming around downtown over the weekend when there were other people here taking care of you. But now you're doing your best to avoid them, and I'm the only person feeding you."

The cat sent me an extremely foul look. "And whose fault is that?"

"Mine," I replied, taking care to keep my tone level. "And once I feel comfortable trying to cast another spell to take care of this whole talking thing, maybe you won't have to worry about it anymore. In the meantime, though, it just makes sense for you to come home with me."

Tilly's long black tail lashed back and forth. "I don't want to be cooped up in a stuffy old house all weekend!"

Well, okay, my house was old, but I didn't think it was stuffy. As for being cooped up—

"I'm going to be home, so I can let you out as often as you want," I told her. "The backyard is really nice, and—"

"I don't want to be cooped up in a yard, either."

For about the millionth time, I cursed myself for being stupid enough to try casting a talking spell on the cat. If Tilly had offered up even the tiniest piece of useful information so far, I might have felt different about the whole thing, but as it was, the situation had been a dumpster fire from beginning to end.

"All right," I replied, trying not to sound too desperate. "You can wander around the neighborhood. Just promise you won't go too far."

Even as I spoke, I hoped I wasn't shooting

myself in the foot. Yes, my neighborhood was pretty quiet, and the chances of Tilly getting hit by a car or encountering some other misfortune were probably lower than they'd be if she stuck around downtown. Once again, I reminded myself that she'd been on the street for years, and she should be able to handle herself just fine.

A long moment while the cat considered my offer, and then she said grudgingly, "All right. As long as I can go out."

"I don't see any reason why you shouldn't," I said.

Unless we had an unseasonable downpour, or....

I told myself to stop borrowing trouble. Another awkward moment as the cat appeared to think things over once again, and then she responded, "It's a deal, then."

Thank God.

And sure, I might have been fibbing a teensy bit when I'd said I would be home, considering my plans to go out with Deanne tonight, but I considered that little white lie only a minor stretching of the truth at best. Besides, even if I'd only intended to stay home and watch TV, I still wouldn't have allowed Tilly to roam the streets after dark.

That was why, after Deanne and I got the shop closed up for the weekend, I gathered all of Tilly's supplies, including her bed and litter box, and put them in the cargo area of my Subaru. The cat followed me outside after I locked up, and then grudgingly jumped into the passenger seat when I opened the car door for her.

Deanne watched all this with amusement but didn't comment, since I'd told her about my arrangement with Tilly. She only said, "See you at seven," and climbed into her RAV4.

I got into my car and started the ignition while the cat gave me a poisonous stare. "Why is she seeing you later?"

"Because we're going out," I said serenely as I began to back out of my parking space and into the alley. "It's my birthday."

"I don't care what day it is," Tilly retorted. "You said you were staying home."

"I am...mostly," I replied. "We're going out tonight, but I'll be home before midnight. I wouldn't have let you out after dark anyway."

The cat appeared to stew in her juices for a moment or two. Then she said, "I go out after dark all the time."

"In a neighborhood you know," I told her. "This is different."

Tilly's nose twitched, but apparently she couldn't come up with a satisfactory rejoinder to my comment, because she lapsed into a sulky silence after that exchange.

Relieved, I headed for home and pulled up in

the driveway a few minutes later. As I went around to the passenger side to let the cat out, I found myself wishing I had a carrier for her. At least that way, I wouldn't have had to worry about her bolting the second I opened the door.

But apparently she'd decided to be on her best behavior, or maybe she'd realized she was in unfamiliar territory here and so it would better to be cautious...at least in the beginning. She followed me primly through the gate and up the back steps, then came inside the kitchen and sent a brief look around.

"It's nice," she said, sounding almost surprised.

Considering Levitation Latte wasn't exactly a dive, I didn't know why Tilly would think I lived in a hovel.

Maybe it was the Subaru. I really needed to do something about that at some point.

"Go ahead and explore," I told her. "I need to go get your stuff out of the car."

Tail in the air, she padded out of the kitchen and into the dining room without bothering to respond.

Fine, then.

I went back outside and got her food, bed, and litter box supplies, and lugged them all up the back steps. The litter box went into the laundry room, while I found a cozy little spot in one corner of the kitchen for her bowls. By the time she returned to the space, I had fresh water and food set out for her.

She went over to them and sniffed, but didn't seem too inclined to start eating right then.

"I want to see the backyard," she said.

You didn't say the magic word, I thought, but rather than trying to correct her manners, I just went over to the kitchen door and let her out. "Scratch when you want back in," I said, and one ear swiveled slightly in my direction, the only acknowledgment I got before she minced her way down the steps and into the yard.

Yep, after this I was definitely getting a dog.

With Tilly handled for the time being, though, I glanced over at the clock on the stove.

A little past four-thirty.

Which gave me oodles of time to get ready for our girls' night out...not that I was planning to go overboard. We weren't going to have champagne at the Ritz or anything quite so posh, so I mostly just wanted to change into clean clothes, put on some makeup, and see if I could do anything with my mane of wavy hair, which tended to be a daunting prospect at the best of times.

First, though, I needed to wait until the cat wanted to be let back in. I could only imagine her ire if I went upstairs to start getting ready and missed her signal to come back inside.

So I made some tea—refreshing peppermint,

nothing I would use to read leaves—and puttered around a little bit, surveying the pantry to see if I needed to make a trip to the store over the weekend, wondering if I should make a batch of cookies or maybe cupcakes the next day, something special that would remind me this was my birthday weekend.

Eventually, Tilly returned and scratched at the back door, and I put down my mug and let her in.

"How was the yard?" I asked pleasantly, and her tail flicked back and forth.

"Adequate," she replied, and then walked out of the kitchen, no doubt headed toward the living room so she could leave cat hairs all over my new couch.

But whatever. That was what vacuum attachments were for. Once I'd determined she was settled—and, to be fair, she'd actually lain down on the rug under the coffee table rather than planting herself on something upholstered—I headed upstairs.

I might have had plenty of time, but I still needed to figure out what to wear that would be comfortable and yet signal at the same time that I was going out for a special occasion.

"Love it," Deanne said as I locked the front door behind me. Once again, Tilly was snoozing on the floor in the living room, and didn't look too put out that I was abandoning her for the evening. Then again, that could have had something to do with the can of tuna I'd given her for dinner, and the salmon treat that had followed.

Hey, I wasn't above bribery if it made life flow a little more smoothly.

I glanced down at myself. "You don't think it's too much?"

At once, she shook her head. "No, you look great. Max is going to kick himself for missing out on this."

Somehow, I doubted that. Yes, I'd put on my sleekest pair of jeans and black ankle boots, and wore a slim leather jacket over a black T-shirt and thought I was looking pretty good, but even so, I had to believe Max was experiencing diversions in L.A. that were a lot more exciting than grabbing burgers at The Skillet and then going out to a dive bar.

But whatever. This night wasn't about him, it was about me.

I didn't respond directly to my friend's comment and only said, "Well, let's get going."

As promised, Mike was behind the wheel of Deanne's Toyota, and flashed us a grin as we climbed inside. "Your chariot awaits, ladies. Where to?"

Deanne shook her head at him. "You know we're going to The Skillet."

He just grinned and put the little SUV in reverse, and backed us out of the driveway. Our destination wasn't very far away, and so he stopped on the street in front of the restaurant just a couple of minutes later. "Call me when you're done," he told Deanne, and she leaned over and kissed him on the cheek.

"Will do."

Since it felt weird to have him drop us off like that, I ventured, "You're sure you don't want to come inside and have dinner with us?"

"Nope," he said cheerfully. "This is your girls' night out. I've got a couple of frozen burritos waiting for me at home. Like I said, just call when you're ready to head to the next stop."

Frozen burritos didn't sound like a very exciting meal for a Friday night, but I knew better than to raise any further objections. "Thanks, Mike," I said.

He gave me a thumbs-up, and then Deanne and I both got out of the car. I didn't know whether she'd called ahead and made special arrangements because it was my birthday or what, but there was a booth waiting for us at a time when the restaurant was usually packed. I took a seat and then told Deanne what I wanted, since it was the sort of place where you had to stand in line at the counter to place your order.

A few minutes later, she was back. "You're sure you don't want a glass of wine?" she asked as she slid a large plastic cup of ice water toward me.

"Definitely sure," I told her. "If I start drinking now, Mike's going to have to carry me out of Blackie's on a stretcher."

She grinned. "Well, we don't want that," she said, then lifted her own glass. "Happy birthday."

I touched my cup against hers, trying to ignore the old wives' tale that said you weren't supposed to toast with plain water. Maybe I could consider this a down payment on future toasts.

Despite the restaurant being packed, our food came quickly enough—a cheeseburger for me and an assortment of tacos for Deanne—and we chatted about nothing in particular as we ate and people-watched. She'd probably decided it wasn't really safe to discuss a talking cat in such a crowded place, and also figured talking about Tom Gallegos' murder was a no-no, too.

Or at least, talking about trying to solve the crime was pretty much off the table. So far, it didn't seem as if anyone had guessed I was trying to track down the mayor's murderer in my own peculiar way, and I wanted to make sure that particular secret didn't leak out.

Not that I was doing such a great job of figuring out who'd sent Tom Gallegos on to the next plane of existence. At the rate I was going, Chief DeVargas would locate the perp and have him locked up before I got a single solitary clue that was of any use.

After dinner, Deanne pulled out her phone and sent off a quick text, obviously letting Mike know it was time to come pick us up. We slipped out of our booth and headed to the curb in front of the restaurant so we could wait there and let someone else have the table.

It was chillier that night than I'd expected, and so I was glad of the leather jacket I'd slipped over my long-sleeved T-shirt. Not too much farther into the month from now, even that jacket might not have been enough, but it worked for the moment.

Mike appeared in what felt like record time, and paused in front of a fire hydrant—the only available space on the block—so Deanne and I could quickly pile in. Since he knew we were headed to Blackie's after this, he asked a quick question about how our dinner had been, and then pointed the RAV4 down to CanAm Highway and the bar that was our destination.

And when he dropped us off, she told him she'd text again when we were ready to leave.

"It'll definitely be before midnight," I added, and she sent me a disgusted look.

"Party pooper."

"Hey, you got me out of the house, didn't you?"

Since she couldn't really argue that particular point, she just shrugged and leaned in to give Mike another kiss. "Okay, we probably won't be too late. Just make sure to keep the phone close by in case you fall asleep while watching Netflix."

"I never—" he began, and Deanne grinned.

"Oh, yes, you do," she broke in. "And you snore. But whatever."

She linked her arm with mine and pulled me toward the entrance to Blackie's. As we went, I found myself wondering if Max ever fell asleep in front of the TV, and whether he snored.

Even if he did, I knew I wouldn't mind...too much. I'd just like to have the opportunity to find out whether he was a snorer or not.

The music that met my ears as Deanne opened the door to Blackie's for me sounded vaguely familiar, and as we made our way into the dimly lit interior, I suddenly realized why.

That was Kyle's band up on stage, wailing their way through a pretty decent rendition of "Sweet Child of Mine."

Deanne sent me a puzzled look. "I thought they already played this week."

"They did," I replied, doing my best to quash

the impulse to turn around and run back out the door.

Stupid of me, I knew. But I really didn't want Kyle getting any ideas about me being here on my birthday.

And even though the interior of the bar was positively cave-like, it wasn't so big that the members of the band couldn't see who was in the audience, especially since the only open table Deanne and I could find was just a row back from the platform where the band was playing. As soon as we sat down, Kyle's eyes tracked straight toward me, like he was a magnet and I was a big old lump of iron.

Great.

Luckily, he wasn't so distracted that he flubbed the lyrics, and so Deanne and I were able to order a couple of rum and Cokes without too much incident. I honestly wasn't a huge rum drinker, but I knew better than to try ordering a glass of wine in a place like Blackie's.

It seemed as though we'd arrived in the middle of a set, because the band moved on to play "Up on Cripple Creek" and then "Harvest Moon" before they finally appeared ready to take a break. Unfortunately, almost as soon as Kyle slipped off his guitar, he made a beeline for our table.

"Mind if I sit down?" he asked, eyeing the two empty chairs.

Since refusing his request would have been extremely rude, I essayed a smile and said, "Sure."

The noise level in the bar had gone down a good bit as soon as the band stopped playing, although the sound system had immediately started piping in a country song, one I didn't recognize. Unfortunately, it wasn't loud enough to prevent us from talking.

Deanne, to my relief, came to my rescue just as soon as Kyle sat down. "So, two gigs in one week? That's pretty cool."

He practically beamed, an expression that warred with his untucked Johnny Cash–style black shirt and torn jeans. "Well, Bad Moon was supposed to be playing tonight, but their lead singer got tonsillitis, so Dawn called me and asked if we could cover their set tonight."

"Good thing you weren't on duty," I said, and then took a sip of my rum and Coke.

A hitch of his shoulders under the black cowboy shirt. "I actually was," Kyle replied, "but I was able to switch with someone. I've been on night shift all week."

Which explained why I hadn't seen him. And here I'd been worried that I'd said something to keep him away.

I should have known it wouldn't be that easy.

"It's great you got someone to take your shift," Deanne said, and drank some of her own rum concoction. "Thinking of quitting and playing full-time?"

Kyle sent her a lopsided grin, as if he wasn't quite sure whether she was teasing him or not. "Nah," he replied. "Being a deputy has better benefits."

I had no doubt about that. For the past couple of years, I'd been skating along with the cheapest public exchange plan I could find, all the while praying I wouldn't have any major health issues to deal with. No reason why I should—my grandmother always said I was healthy as a horse—but accidents happened no matter how careful you were.

"Hey, Kyle," I said, trying my best to sound casual, and not sure whether I was really succeeding, since I had to talk a little louder than normal to be heard over the music in the background, "any new developments in the Tom Gallegos case?"

At once, Kyle's grin faded. However, since he didn't look particularly wary, I guessed his newly grim expression had more to do with the police department's lack of progress in finding Tom's killer than because I was getting too nosy.

"Not really," he said. "I mean, it sounds like there's a ton of evidence to comb through, stuff that was found on the scene. Nothing that's conclusive, unfortunately, mostly because so many people were coming and going in the park that night. The M.E. said Tom Gallegos died sometime between six and seven, so that seems to indicate he was killed somewhere else and dumped in the maze, since you didn't stumble across his body until almost seven-thirty, Skye. We already kind of knew that, though, since there's no physical evidence to show he was actually killed in the maze, and the medical examiner says there were indications that rigor mortis had begun to set in before he was moved." Kyle reached up to scratch the back of his head and then shrugged. "Whoever did it, they definitely knew how to cover their tracks."

Apparently so. God knows the tea leaves weren't giving me anything to work with.

Would this end up a cold case, something shoved to the back of a filing cabinet after weeks or even months of investigation didn't turn up a single useful clue? I knew it happened sometimes, probably more than the police would like to admit. And maybe even more likely in a place like Las Vegas, which didn't exactly have a bunch of world-class homicide detectives in its ranks. No doubt Chief DeVargas and the rest of her team were doing the best they could, but maybe their best wasn't quite good enough.

"But," Kyle added, and my ears pricked up right away, "there was one weird thing."

"What's that?" Deanne asked, obviously doing her best to match my previous laid-back tone.

He glanced around, but no one was paying any attention to us. The crowd that night was a mixture of people I recognized from our high school days—probably here to lend Kyle moral support—and quite a few couples old enough to be our parents' age who probably didn't care what the band was playing as long as they could get out of the house for a few hours and have a couple of drinks. And, as in every other lounge I'd ever visited, there was that one guy sitting at the end of the bar, someone who was clearly three sheets to the wind and looked as though he might have wandered in after spending forty years roaming the desert.

"Well," Kyle said, apparently having convinced himself that no one was trying to eavesdrop on our conversation, "you know the girl who was taking tickets at the corn maze, Lisbeth Gilbert?"

I actually didn't know the high school student by name, although she'd dropped into Levitation Latte with groups of friends from time to time. However, I only nodded, figuring there was no point in getting bogged down in minutiae.

"She told Chief DeVargas that someone contacted her on the walkie-talkie to let her know the last group that had gone through the maze had spilled their sodas and a bunch of popcorn toward the end, and so they didn't want her letting anyone else in until it had been cleaned up. She got the all-clear right before you and Max showed up."

Okay, that wasn't fishy at all. Deanne shot a significant glance in my direction, showing she'd also just put two and two together and wasn't too happy with the result.

"Does Maddie know who was on the walkie-talkie?" I asked.

Kyle shook his head. "No," he replied. "She said it was a man, but she didn't recognize his voice. That wasn't too weird, since there were a lot of volunteers at the festival, and anyone who was working security or logistics would have been given a walkie-talkie. The thing is, we questioned all of them, and they all denied making that call to Maddie."

Which meant one of them must have been lying...or had loaned their walkie-talkie to someone else so they could get in touch with the girl standing guard at the entrance to the corn maze. And with the coast cleared for as long as they needed, that meant it wouldn't have been too diffi-cult to drop Tom Gallegos' body into the maze—probably from the side that faced Gonzales Street, since it would have been easier to make a quick getaway from that location—and be long gone before Max and I came along.

"Well, someone was lying," Deanne said

frankly, and Kyle shrugged, now looking uncomfortable.

"Maybe," he allowed. "But I find that kind of hard to believe. I saw the witness list—it was a bunch of people we all know, friends and neighbors or whatever. None of them seem the type to cover up a murder."

I noticed how Kyle had been careful not to name any names. That made sense, though—he was willing to fill me in on the details up to a point, but no way in the world would he come right out and divulge who was and wasn't a person of interest in the case. And I also guessed from his slightly worried expression that he feared he'd already let slip just a little too much.

"That's really interesting, Kyle," I said. "We really appreciate you keeping us in the loop."

At once, his expression turned to one of relief. It seemed obvious to me he'd been afraid that I might continue to press him for more information. "Anyway," he said, "happy birthday, Skye! I feel kind of honored that you came here to celebrate."

Because I didn't think you'd be playing tonight, went through my mind, but I dismissed that sour observation. It was just like Kyle to have remembered the day, even though we'd only gone out for about six months, and now almost a year had passed since our breakup. He paid attention to stuff like that, and on my birthday had driven me to Santa Fe for a special dinner at a place called Sazon, an outing that I knew had cost him a pretty penny.

If only I could get past our complete lack of chemistry. Was it really all that big a deal? Wasn't having someone around who appreciated you and was friendly and easygoing a lot more important?

For some people, maybe. Unfortunately, it seemed as though my unrequited crush on Max Sullivan was going to haunt me until the day I died. Kyle might have looked good on paper, but I knew he wasn't the one. Not for me, anyway.

"Oh, well," I said, trying to think of a way to respond to his remark while not calling Blackie's out for the dive bar it was. "I just wanted to go someplace where I could let my hair down."

"And it looks great," he replied, eyeing my long, wavy locks.

To be fair, they were cooperating that night, mostly because I'd spent over an hour doing my best to tame them with heat styling lotion and a big-barrel curling iron. The results weren't as professional-looking as Deanne's careless beachy waves, mostly because she had a knack for working with hair while I didn't, but at least I didn't look like a complete bramble bush.

"So, how many sets are you playing tonight?" she asked then, obviously noting the awkward silence that had fallen after Kyle's uninvited compliment.

"Oh, three," he said. To my relief, it didn't seem as if he'd recognized the red herring for what it was, and had taken her question at face value. "We'll be playing until at least one, maybe later."

"And I'll definitely turn into a pumpkin before that," I told him. "But we'll stick around as long as we can."

One of Kyle's bandmates called out to him then, looking as though he wanted to discuss something before they started their next set. Obviously reluctant, he got up from his chair and said, "Well, it was nice to see you here tonight. Let me know if you have any requests."

Fat chance. I swallowed some more of my rum and Coke and muttered...after Kyle was safely out of earshot, "My only request is to be somewhere else."

Deanne pursed her lips for a moment, and had some of her drink as well. "Do you want to go? We can head over to the bar at the Plaza or something if you want to get out of here."

For just a second or two, I seriously considered her request. Then I realized how bad it would look to Kyle if we got up and left as soon as he'd vacated his seat at our table.

"No, that's okay," I said. "I mean, I already let Kyle know we weren't going to stick around all night. Let's stay for the next set and see what happens."

She looked skeptical at first, and then shrugged, as if reminding herself that it was my birthday and so I needed to be the one calling the shots.

And maybe this hadn't been a complete waste of time. At least now I knew Kyle had been working night shift all week, that Tom Gallegos had definitely died sometime between six and seven last Saturday night, and that an unknown person had made sure the corn maze would be unoccupied while they dumped their grisly burden there. What it all exactly meant, I didn't know for sure, but there were definitely several pieces of information I hadn't possessed before now.

A couple of pieces out of thousands. I had to wonder how long it would take to collect the rest of them.

CHAPTER 14

Gossip Girl

Deanne and I stuck around for most of the band's second set, but any desire to party hearty had pretty much disappeared. I knew Kyle was concentrating on the music and not watching me every second or anything close to that, and yet I knew I was way too self-conscious to get up and dance with my friend the way I might have if the band had been some safely anonymous group from Santa Fe or Taos or whatever.

As it was, we ordered another round of drinks, sort of limped our way through a half-hearted conversation as we watched Kyle and his bandmates play, and ended up calling Mike to come get us a little before eleven. When he arrived, I could tell he was surprised to be picking us up so early. However, he took one look at Deanne's face and probably decided it was safer not to ask too many questions.

When they dropped me off at home, I gave Deanne's hand a quick squeeze—trying to hug her over the seat back would have been difficult, if not impossible—and said, "I had a great time. Thanks so much for taking me out tonight."

Her lopsided smile in response to those words indicated she knew I was lying through my teeth. But, good friend that she was, she knew to just accept my thanks and put an end to the evening. "Oh, it was fun! And happy birthday."

I smiled back at her and at Mike, then got out of the car and headed inside. Tilly was right there in the living room—on the sofa, naturally—and shot me a quizzical look as I locked the door.

"You didn't have to come home so early on my account," she said, and I sent her a pained glance.

"I didn't," I said. "But Deanne and I have been up since four-thirty, so we both decided to call it a night."

Well, part of that was true. We had both been awake since before the crack of dawn, but it wasn't weariness that had compelled us to call it a night. Once upon a time, I would have been dancing and tossing back rum and Cokes until at least two in the morning.

Maybe I really was getting old.

No, that wasn't it. My energy levels were just

fine. The only reason Deanne and I had bailed out early was that I couldn't let my hair down—figuratively speaking—and allow myself to really go crazy with Kyle watching me.

Also, my brain had kept churning away at the details about the murder investigation he'd spilled to the two of us, and I knew I needed some quiet time to sit and ponder what it all meant.

Tilly's whiskers twitched, and I got the distinct impression she knew I wasn't exactly telling her the truth. To my relief, however, she didn't seem interested in questioning me further, but only curled herself back up into a ball and closed her eyes. It looked as though she planned to stay there on the couch all night, never mind that she had a perfectly good bed waiting for her on the floor next to the fireplace.

But whatever.

I headed into the kitchen, thinking that a cup of chamomile tea might be just the thing I needed right then. While I hadn't gotten anywhere close to drunk—even though the second rum and Coke had been a lot stronger than the first—I still knew I needed to hydrate and get something in my system that wasn't quite so toxic.

Filling the kettle and waiting for the water to boil calmed me a little, the familiar routine helping to smooth out my jangling thoughts. However, even as I waited for my tea to cool so I could drink it, one question kept thrumming in my mind.

Had the mysterious person on the walkie-talkie only given the all-clear because he'd seen Max and me approaching?

On the surface, that theory didn't make much sense. It could have all been a coincidence.

But....

Max had been accused of murder just the month before. He'd been cleared of all charges, of course, but that only went so far. There were probably people out there who still thought he must be guilty, that he'd used his money and influence to clear his name. What if the murderer—or their accomplice, since I didn't know the identity of the man on the walkie-talkie, and realized he might not have been the actual killer—had given the all-clear to Lisbeth Gilbert exactly because he wanted Max Sullivan to stumble onto the body? The ensuing furor might have been enough to muddy the waters, if nothing else.

Except that hadn't happened. Chief DeVargas was the stereotypical tough but fair cop, and she'd realized at once that Max had nothing to do with Tom Gallegos' death.

In this particular instance, the killer had definitely swung for the fences and missed, but it looked as though they were going to make it to home plate regardless, since none of the clues unearthed so far had done anything to reveal their identity.

I blew on my chamomile tea, wishing for about the thousandth time that Max was here so I could discuss these theories with him and see what he thought. But he was a thousand miles away and wouldn't be back until Sunday afternoon, so until then, I was on my own.

Not completely, of course. I knew that Deanne would be all too happy to pick apart Kyle's revelations to see if we could come up with anything of substance.

But because we spent all week together at the shop, I did my best to let her share her weekends with Mike and not interfere too much. If I'd cultivated a few more female friendships in town, I might have had someone else to chat with. Unfortunately, the scars from my high school years made it hard for me to recognize that some of those girls might have changed over the intervening decade, and that it might have been okay to try getting close to someone besides Deanne Daniels.

I tried to reassure myself that it was fine. There was plenty for me to do around the house tomorrow, and Max would be back on Sunday. It wouldn't kill me to wait for his return.

Or at least, that was what I told myself.

But Saturday actually zoomed past more quickly than I'd thought it would, mostly because I did whatever I could to keep myself busy. I did laundry and cleaned the house and went to the store, and then made a batch of peanut butter chocolate chip cookies to cheer myself up. True, I rationalized the cookies by making a vow to take at least half of them over to Max's house after he got home the next day so I wouldn't end up eating all three dozen of them by myself over the course of the next week, but still, it felt like a good use of my time.

And the day got even better after he sent me a text around three, letting me know that he should be back in Las Vegas around four the next afternoon.

Early dinner at The Skillet? he asked. *My treat.*

Any meal with him was his treat, because he'd never once let me pick up the tab, even when I'd protested that there needed to be some kind of equity involved when we went out to eat. Of course, he was a multi-millionaire and I wasn't, so maybe trying to keep things even was a waste of energy.

Sure, I wrote back. *I've got lots to tell you.*

Can't wait, he sent back. *I'll text you tomorrow —see you then.*

I sent him a thumbs-up emoji, and that was the end of the conversation.

Still, I was in a much better mood for the rest

of the afternoon, even if the extra bits and pieces of clues that Kyle had given me didn't want to resolve themselves into a complete picture. My brain kept picking at the problem as I thought of what Lucy Margolis had told me about the way she'd seen Raylene talking to the mayor and looking way too intimate. But as much as I might have wanted Raylene involved somehow, my brain couldn't quite convince itself that I was on the right track.

I finished the laundry and the house was spotless, and so I felt justified in sitting in front of the TV that night and watching utterly mindless fluff. And Tilly seemed to be in a fairly good mood—well, as good as her moods ever got—mostly because I'd been around to let her in and out as often as she liked. After dinner, she even curled up in her bed so I'd have the sofa to myself, and all in all, I had to admit it had been a pretty good day.

And the next one would be even better, because Max was coming home.

Did he think of Las Vegas as home? Did his place back in Bel-Air now feel as if it belonged to someone else?

For all I knew, part of the "business" he was handling with his assistant was finally deciding to put the place on the market, even though he hadn't come out and said such a thing.

Maybe that was wishful thinking, though. Just because he seemed settled at the ranch didn't mean he intended to live there permanently. After all, he'd bought it less than a month ago.

But I didn't want to think about any of that. I pushed the unwelcome thoughts from my mind so I could focus on the positive.

This time tomorrow, we'd be having dinner together.

Once again, I had what appeared to be a dreamless night, and once again, I couldn't help feeling a little irritated. If having prophetic dreams was one of my gifts, then when was the universe going to get its act together and actually send me one?

I wouldn't let myself worry about that too much, though. It was far more important to spend just as much time on my hair today as I had for Deanne's and my ill-fated girls' night out on Friday, and to pick out something to wear that was effortless and flattering at the same time. For a moment or two, I contemplated wearing the gorgeous cashmere sweater she'd gotten me for my birthday, but the weather wasn't really cold enough yet for that.

Instead, I settled for a long-sleeved black T-shirt with some cute folkloric-looking appliqués that I'd bought in Santa Fe a while back, and my favorite black ankle boots and a well-broken-in pair of jeans. Nothing too fancy, but also a little more interesting than a plain shirt would have been.

And after doing some research on new muffin flavors I wanted to introduce for the holidays—eggnog with streusel topping and bacon maple topped the list of my test recipes—I got another text from Max around four-thirty.

Flight was delayed a bit, he wrote, *but I just landed in Albuquerque. Can I swing by & get you a little before 7?*

Airline delays were a fact of life for pretty much everyone, so I couldn't be too annoyed about Max showing up later than we'd originally planned. I wrote back, *Sounds good. I'll be ready.*

See you then.

That was all, but at least he hadn't begged off because the flight was late and he was worn out.

Then again, I didn't think I'd ever seen Max Sullivan beg off from anything just because he was too tired to attend. He wasn't the kind of person who got tired. Maybe a little deflated if things weren't going his way—like when he'd been accused of Perry Lockhart's murder—but downright exhausted?

Never.

Seven o'clock felt way too far off, but I kept myself busy by watching more TV, since I was too antsy to try reading anything. Tilly seemed amused by my restlessness, although, since I was more than happy to burn off extra energy by getting up and letting her out at regular intervals, she didn't deign to comment.

At last I saw a pair of headlights pull up into the driveway a little after seven. Running about ten minutes late, which was par for the course for Max.

But I reminded myself that he'd just driven up from Albuquerque, and probably hadn't stopped at his house to do anything except drop off his luggage.

Wanting to save him from having to get out of the car and come up the porch steps to the front door, I slipped my purse over my shoulder and let myself out, pausing briefly to lock up the house. I'd already put on my black leather jacket, so I didn't have to worry about wasting time doing that.

It seemed Max had caught sight of me coming out of the house, because he remained behind the wheel, engine running. A moment later, I opened the passenger-side door and climbed into the Bronco.

"I could've come up and knocked," he said, his tone faintly accusing.

"I know," I replied as I fastened my seatbelt. "But you've already had a long day, so I thought I'd save you the trouble."

Maybe just the faintest shake of his head before he began to back out of the driveway. "It wasn't too bad. The worst part was getting stuck on the runway in Phoenix for almost an hour."

Yes, that would be annoying. I swiveled in my seat so I could face him more directly and remarked, "I'm surprised you don't have a private jet."

Now he grinned. "I won't say I haven't thought about it—especially now I'm living some-where that's super-close to a general aviation airport. Before, it just seemed easier to have the studios fly me wherever they wanted me to go." A pause as his eyes crinkled with amusement. "I guess I forgot how it's almost impossible to get a direct flight from Albuquerque to anywhere important."

Since I'd never been out of the state—well, except a quick jaunt to Denver one time and another to El Paso right before my grandmother died several years ago—I couldn't really comment on that. I'd often thought wistfully about travel-ing...*really* traveling...but even though I'd gotten a passport just in case, the demands of running my own business seemed to preclude ever being able to make my escape.

Whereas Max had traveled all over the world while shooting all those films and TV shows. A flicker of jealousy went through me, one I tried to quickly quell. Comparing my life to his was a recipe for disaster. Besides, hadn't I told him the night of the harvest festival that I was satisfied with my life and didn't really need anything more than what I already had?

"Then you should definitely get a private jet," I said firmly.

"I still have to have someone to fly it," he returned, and I just smiled.

"What, you don't know how to fly a jet?"

"No, but I've faked it pretty well on camera."

I chuckled, and he slid the Bronco into an open space right in front of the restaurant. True, it was a Sunday night, and so The Skillet wasn't as busy as it might otherwise have been, but even so, I couldn't reflect on the remarkable luck that seemed to follow my friend wherever he went.

Luck that held as we went into the restaurant and discovered one of the prime tables by the window was open. A few people seemed to do a double take as we walked up to the counter to place our orders, but no one acted so starstruck that we couldn't ignore them.

Which was probably about as much as we could hope for.

After we'd both sat down at our table with our glasses of water—someone would be by with Max's beer and my glass of wine soon enough—I said, "So, it sounds like someone on the inside must have killed Tom Gallegos."

Max blinked at me but wasn't able to reply right away, since a server came over and deposited our drinks, letting us know the food would be out shortly. I recognized the guy—his name was Steve Williamson, and he'd been a class behind me in high school—but I didn't do anything except murmur a thank-you, since I didn't want any more distractions from my conversation with my companion.

After we'd both had a fortifying sip from our drinks, Max said, "Why would you think it's an inside job?"

I gave him a brief summary of what Kyle had told me at Blackie's on Friday night, concluding with, "So, it had to be someone who was working at the festival, or they wouldn't have been able to contact Maddie through her walkie-talkie."

To my surprise, Max looked dubious. "I'm not so sure about that."

"What do you mean, you're not sure?"

He shrugged and reached for his glass of brown ale. "Because it's not as if walkie-talkie frequencies are private. Someone could have known the people working the festival would be using walkie-talkies to keep in contact with each other and just figured out which band they were using."

Oh. I hadn't even thought of that, mostly because I'd never had any reason to use one of the little radios. Max, on the other hand, would have been around walkie-talkies all the time on movie sets, even if he himself might not have needed to carry one.

"But it's still possible the killer could be one of the people working the festival," I persisted.

"Of course it's possible," he replied. "I'm just saying it's not the only possibility."

Damn. And here I'd thought I was really on to something.

Steve came over with our food and asked if we needed anything. After we both said we were good, he headed back toward the counter, leaving Max and me alone again.

"But it's definitely an important piece of information," he went on, as though he could tell I was disappointed by the realization that I might not be as close to solving the mystery as I would have liked and he wanted to do what he could to cheer me up.

I lifted one of my carnitas tacos and took a bite. Yes, that was just what the doctor ordered. It was always easier to feel better about life when I was eating a Skillet taco.

"Maybe," I allowed after I was done chewing. "But I'm still trying to figure out why the killer would want us to find the body."

Max was in the middle of making a serious dent in his cheeseburger, leading me to believe he hadn't eaten much—if anything—while on the plane. Once he was done chewing, he responded, "Like you said, it was a distraction. One that didn't work, but I suppose we should give them points for trying."

Right then, I was in no mood to be teased, mostly because I couldn't shake the feeling that the answer was right under my nose and I was too stupid to see it. Maybe I shouldn't have been so hard on myself...it wasn't as if I had any training in this sort of thing, and it didn't seem as though the police were doing much better...but if nothing else, Tom Gallegos deserved to have his murderer brought to justice, and his grieving family needed to have closure.

But because I could tell Max was only trying to cheer me up, I managed a wan smile and replied, "Yeah, I guess that was one piece of spaghetti they threw at the wall that didn't exactly stick."

As I'd hoped, he grinned at my comment, and then steered the conversation toward safer topics, like what I planned to do for Halloween. I told him I was a little old for trick-or-treating, but again, he only smiled.

"Are you too old for a costume party at my place?"

When I was a kid, I'd loved dressing up for Halloween, mainly because it gave me an excuse to pretend to be someone else for an evening. Now, though, I just slanted Max a sideways glance and inquired, "Isn't this kind of short notice for a Halloween party? It's less than two weeks away."

"Like it matters," he replied, leaning against the back of his chair before allowing himself a sip of his beer. "You know I could send out the invites two days before and still have a full house."

Since that was only the truth, I lifted my shoulders. "Then okay, a Halloween party sounds like fun."

Even as I spoke, I wondered what I would wear to a get-together like that. Should I surprise everyone and show up in something sexy, or should I play it safe and just wear a witch hat and a black dress?

Everyone already thought I was something of a witch, so it wouldn't be as though I was defying expectations.

"Then I'll start planning it," Max said. His expression was supremely confident, as though he had no doubt he would pull off the party of the year even if he only had ten days or so to get it together.

Well, of course he'd be able to do something like that. He had practically unlimited funds to back him up...and I had no doubt he'd probably rope his assistant into handling any logistics that weren't interesting or fun enough to merit his own attention.

In a way, I was glad. Thinking about a Halloween party would help to distract us both from our dismal lack of progress in the Gallegos murder case.

Not entirely, though. I knew I didn't plan to give up...even if our chances weren't looking very good at the moment.

What else could I do?

CHAPTER 15

Blood Brothers

That night, I dreamed.

At first, the image I saw seemed completely innocuous. Two little dark-haired boys were playing in a large grassy yard, first just chasing each other around, and then climbing all over a large wooden fort type of structure, the kind of expensive thing with a slide and a rope ladder and monkey bars that Max had in his backyard when he was a kid.

But I knew Max's hair had been bright blond when he was a boy, darkening to its current light brown as he got older, and both of the children in my dream were much darker than that, with hair nearly black and brown eyes. They climbed up the rope ladders and slid down the slide, hung off the monkey bars, and clambered up the rope ladder so they could do it all over again.

Until....

Both boys were standing on top of the fort, apparently pretending to survey their backyard kingdom. The younger of the two stood a little ways behind his older brother and cracked a huge grin.

Then he reached out with both hands to push his brother off the top of the fort.

The thud he made when he hit the ground was so horrible, I sat upright in bed, heart racing, cold sweat dripping down my back even though my room was warm enough, thanks to the central heat my grandmother had installed years ago to replace the old-fashioned radiators. For a second or two, I just sat there, hands braced against the mattress, as I tried my best to erase that sickening sound from my mind.

No such luck, though. The dream had been incredibly vivid, so real it felt almost like one of my own memories, even though I knew I'd never seen those two little boys before.

Or...had I?

Sitting there in the darkness, I wracked my brains, trying to recall all the kids I'd babysat when I was younger. The Martinez boys came to mind first, but they'd been older when I watched them, eleven and nine, and not completely happy about having some high school girl keeping an eye on them so their parents could have a precious date night from time to time. Also, their features were very different from the boys in my dream, rounder and almost cherubic, whereas those dream-children looked a lot more rascally.

But even though I didn't know who those boys were—or at least, who they were supposed to represent—I could tell the dream was a true one. Otherwise, it wouldn't have been so razor-sharp in every detail, feeling more like something I'd witnessed for myself, rather than simply a dream.

Problem was, I had no idea what it was supposed to mean.

I glanced over at the clock.

1:11 a.m.

Even I knew that the hours of 11:11 and 1:11 were supposed to be significant, at least according to the folk wisdom of those who believed in angelic intervention and signs and portents. That I'd woken up from my dream at exactly eleven minutes after one o'clock told me I couldn't ignore this dream.

"Well, then, give me a sign as to how I'm supposed to interpret the damn thing," I grumbled.

Unfortunately, the universe seemed to think it had done its job by sending me the dream, because I definitely wasn't rewarded with any flashes of insight. And as much as I thought it might help to go downstairs and make myself some chamomile tea, I didn't want to disturb Tilly, who was sleeping on her bed by the fireplace when I headed upstairs to go to sleep.

Also, I had to be up for work in three and a half hours. Getting out of bed and wandering around the house might do more harm than good.

So I rolled over on my side, shut my eyes, and hoped for more illumination in the morning.

No such luck. That is, even after showering, having a cup of coffee, and getting dressed, I wasn't rewarded with any flashes of insight as to who the boys in my dream might have been, or why I kept feeling as though I'd overlooked something.

But because I knew my customers probably wouldn't care that I was having a hard time interpreting my dream, I headed in to work at my usual five-thirty, Tilly and all her accoutrements in tow. As much as I might have preferred leaving her at home, I knew that wasn't an option. No, I had to bring her with me and allow her to roam her beloved downtown Las Vegas.

After I let her out of the car, she sauntered away down the alley, clearly ready to reacquaint herself with any new smells or interesting trash that might have come on the scene during her absence. And because I'd expected as much, I didn't bother to call after her, but only went inside and got a fresh pot of coffee going before heading back into the kitchen to start baking that morning's batches of muffins, croissants, and bagels.

Not too long afterward, Deanne appeared. She glanced around, obviously looking for Tilly.

"Oh, she's out wandering," I said. "But the coffee's ready."

"Thank God," Deanne replied with a grin.

"Rough weekend?" I asked.

"Not unless you call doing laundry 'rough,'" she said. "No, I just feel like I woke up on the wrong side of the bed today, for whatever reason."

"Sounds like a case of the Mondays," I told her. "Which means you need some coffee, stat."

She shot me another smile and then headed out into the main area of the shop so she could begin her usual morning transfusion of caffeine. While she was occupied with that task, I wondered whether I should tell her about my dream, then decided to let it go for now. Its meaning still seemed so vague to me that I doubted she'd be able to shed any light on the subject.

In fact, I vigorously avoided any mention of Tom Gallegos' murder, instead telling Deanne when she came back into the kitchen that Max was planning a Halloween party. She immediately brightened, saying, "Oh, that's a great idea. I haven't been to a party like that in a million years."

Which made sense, considering that a lot of people our age had already started families and were too busy chasing toddlers to worry about throwing a party.

But Max didn't have any toddlers and was clearly looking for ways to keep himself occupied, leading the way for the rest of us to benefit from his constant need for excitement of some kind.

Deanne and I chitchatted about possible costumes while I finished getting that morning's baked goods ready to be popped into the oven and she went about her usual ritual of prepping the shop for our early bird customers.

"I wish we had more time to get ready for Max's party, though," she said wistfully as she refilled one of the napkin containers. "I would have loved to go as Daenerys from *Game of Thrones,* but I doubt I have time to get anything like that together."

Honestly, I thought my cheerful friend was about as different from Daenerys Targaryen in personality as someone could possibly be, but maybe that was the point. Doing my best to be encouraging, I said, "Oh, I don't know. That's probably a pretty popular costume. You might be able to find something online."

Deanne's expression immediately turned thoughtful. "Ooh, I'll have to look that up."

As soon as she was done with the napkin

dispenser, she whipped her phone out of her apron pocket and started doing some research. I smiled to myself but didn't tell her that her internet search needed to wait until later—we were just about ready for that morning's customers, and she would be too busy once the shop opened to have the time to search for the perfect Halloween costume.

And sure enough, she found something on Etsy that would work, and went ahead and put in her order right then and there. I almost told her that maybe she should have waited until Max sent out his formal announcements but decided to keep quiet. If the party fell through for some reason, she could always wear the costume next year.

Once the shop was open, we definitely had enough customers coming and going that the time passed quickly enough. As usual, Deanne and I spelled each other at lunch, with one person holding down the fort for a half-hour while the other hid in the back room and ate her sack lunch —or, in my case today, a ham and cheese croissant that I'd nabbed from the bakery case.

A little after one, though, Deanne's phone rang from inside her apron pocket. She pulled it out, said "hello?" and then waited for a few moments while she listened to the person at the other end of the line. Then she said, "Hang on—let me check," and turned toward me.

"Dr. Sanchez has an opening at three today to

replace my temporary crown," she said. "Do you mind if I duck out early? My real appointment isn't for another week, but if I can go in today—"

"It's fine," I assured her. Which it was, since we were always much busier in the morning than we were in the afternoon, even on the days when we got an influx of high school students coming in right before closing.

And even if it would have been a stretch to keep watch on the shop by myself, I still wouldn't have told her she couldn't go to the dentist. Deanne had gotten her so-called "temporary" crown a month earlier, and making her wait another week just seemed mean.

"Bless you," she breathed, then said into her phone, "I can be there at three. Thanks so much."

With that matter settled, the next two hours passed quickly enough, and at about a quarter 'til, she thanked me again and hurried out. Left alone, I glanced at the clock behind the counter and hoped I wouldn't be inundated with marauding high schoolers. There didn't seem to be any real pattern to when they decided to drop in to Levitation Latte or when they picked some other after-school hangout, like the Dairy Queen or Sonic.

That day, however, it seemed as though they'd decided to descend somewhere else, because I only had Mrs. Carmichael drop by for a chai latte to go...along with a refill on the special turmeric ginger tea she used to keep her arthritis pain under control, a special batch I kept under the counter along with all the other custom-blended teas and elixirs I created for a certain subset of my patrons. Whether or not it was strictly legal for me to be dispensing those items, I wasn't sure, but since I didn't represent them as medicinal—and because I did have a food service license from the state of New Mexico—I guessed I was all right, albeit occupying a sort of gray area.

Around a quarter after three, though, just as I was starting to tidy up and get ready to shut the doors at three-thirty, Cory Sills came in.

She didn't look quite as stressed out as the last time I'd seen her, maybe because, with the special election happening the next day, she'd begun to see a light at the end of the tunnel. As before, she was carrying a stack of flyers with her.

I sent her a smile and then said, "Hey, Cory. I've already got your flyer up in the window."

"Oh, I know," she replied. "I saw it—and thank you for posting it. I just thought I'd bring a few more so you can post them inside the shop somewhere, like on a bathroom door or whatever."

That made sense. It was kind of hard to ignore something that was staring at you from the back of a door opposite the toilet. Plus, I had a message board mounted on the wall next to the bathroom, which would give people another place to see the notice.

"Sure," I said. "I'll take a couple."

Cory came over and handed me three of the flyers, then asked, "Did you get your ballot?"

"I did," I responded. "It was there when I checked the mail Saturday afternoon. You got those out incredibly fast."

While she didn't exactly smile in response to this praise, her expression brightened a bit. "Thanks. It was a concerted effort, that's for sure." A glance up at the clock, and she added, "Well, I won't keep you. Thanks again for posting the flyers where people can see them."

"No problem at all," I assured her, and she nodded, then headed out the door, her stride brisk, as though she knew she had a lot of ground to cover before the day was over.

Because I didn't have any customers at the moment—and had a feeling I wouldn't have any more before I closed everything down in about fifteen minutes—I picked up the flyers and headed toward the back of the shop and the short hallway where the bathrooms were located. As I was pinning one of the sheets of blue paper to the bulletin board, Tilly stuck her head into the hall and sent me a quizzical look.

"Who was that woman?" she asked.

"Cory?" I said, and then continued pinning up the flyer. "She's the mayor's assistant. Why?"

The cat came into the hallway and sat down on her haunches. I'd left the door to the combined kitchen/storeroom open because I was here by myself and needed to go back and forth quickly if I had to fetch something, which was probably why Tilly had overheard my conversation with Cory Sills.

"She lives two streets over from you, right?"

I blinked, wondering how the cat had come into possession of that particular piece of information. But then I reminded myself she'd had most of the weekend to go wandering around my neighborhood, so it didn't seem too strange that she might have roamed as far as Cory's house.

"Yes," I said. "What has that got to do with anything?"

Tilly's big green eyes narrowed a bit. However, apparently she decided that sharing her knowledge was more important than taking offense at my tone, because she said, "I was in her backyard and heard her arguing with a man."

No point in giving Tilly grief for invading someone else's yard. Cats went where they wanted —even talking cats. And Saturday had been unseasonably warm for this time of year, explaining why Cory might have had her windows open. Not all the houses in my neighborhood had been upgraded with central air the way mine had.

"And?" I prompted.

"She and the man were arguing about a clover field," Tilly went on. "It didn't make any sense, because then the man said something about no one ever finding out, and this Cory person told him he hadn't been careful enough. Honestly, their conversation was getting kind of tedious, so I jumped onto the wall and went into her neighbor's yard."

None of this seemed to matter much to Tilly, who'd delivered this information in her usual deadpan tone. As for me, well....

It all fell into place with what felt to me like an audible *click,* albeit a click that seemed to shake me to my core.

The three-leaf clover and the shovel in my tea reading. The two dark-haired little boys, one of them pushed to what appeared to be his death by his younger sibling.

And Cloverfield. Of course.

Okay, that wasn't really its name. The proper name of the place was Jaramillo Field. It was a big piece of land on the northwest side of Las Vegas, land that had once been owned by the Jaramillo family but had been deeded to the city back in the late 1970s. We kids called it Cloverfield because it was covered in—you guessed it—lush purple clover every spring and summer, and was a great place to go fly kites or just run around and get your wiggles out.

And without fail, every few years some developer or another would try to buy the land, and every time would get shot down. Las Vegas wasn't a no-growth kind of place, but it was sort of a tradition among the town's mayors to make sure Jaramillo Field stayed unspoiled...and Tom Gallegos had been very clear about continuing that tradition.

An awful chill went down my spine. The dream seemed all too clear to me now, even though a few hours earlier, I would have laughed at the suspicions that now were churning away in my brain.

Dave Gallegos had killed his older brother to get him out of the way so that land could be developed. All he needed was to become the next mayor, and he'd be able to make sure Jaramillo Field was Cloverfield no more.

And with public sentiment making him pretty much a shoo-in to take over from his brother, it seemed the younger Gallegos would be our mayor in less than forty-eight hours.

The sensible part of my brain rose up as I guessed it would, arguing that I was making a pretty big leap of logic right now, and how there could have been a perfectly reasonable explanation for why Dave and Cory had been arguing about that valuable piece of land.

True enough...except for his remark about getting away with it, and her rejoinder that he hadn't been careful enough.

That all sounded pretty darn incriminating to me.

Why Cory Sills was involved, I had no idea, even as I guessed she must have been the one to supply Dave with a walkie-talkie so he could ensure the corn maze was unoccupied while he dumped his brother's body there.

It looked like I'd been right about the whole thing being an inside job.

"What's the matter?" Tilly asked dryly. "Cat got your tongue?"

I didn't even bother to scowl at her. "Thanks for the information," I told her. "It's been very educational."

"Does that mean you'll give me an extra treat?"

As far as I was concerned, she could have the whole box of them. If she hadn't been roaming around my neighborhood during the weekend and overheard Cory and Dave quarreling, their guilt might have never come to light.

Without replying directly, I went into the storeroom and got the treats down from the shelf, then put three of them on the floor. "You've earned it," I said.

Tilly didn't exactly thank me, but her expression was a little less sour as she bent to scarf up the treats. That bit of business handled, I went back out front.

Once again, I glanced up at the clock.

Three twenty-five. Close enough.

I got out the keys and locked the front door, then performed the world's quickest clean-up, carelessly wiping down tables without paying much attention to whether or not I got every spot, and then merely rinsing out the coffeepots and the espresso maker, figuring I'd do a better job when I came in the next morning.

Right now, though, I needed to figure out what to do next.

Calling Max with my suspicions felt like the most logical course of action. When I pulled out my phone, however, it was to discover I'd missed a text from him.

Have to run back to L.A., it said. *Should be home no later than Tuesday night.*

Well, damn it.

And sure, I could call him even though he was on the West Coast, but I really didn't want to bother him in case he was in the middle of important negotiations. Whatever he was doing had to be important, or he wouldn't have gone back so soon after his last trip.

Deanne also wouldn't be of much help, since I

had to assume she was currently in a dentist's chair and would probably take a while to come down from the Novocain and nitrous cocktail she'd been given while getting her permanent crown put in place.

All right, I needed to think this through logically. I didn't want to say anything to Kyle, just in case Cory actually was an innocent bystander.

Which meant I really needed to talk to her again and see if I could get her to drop even the tiniest piece of incriminating information.

Easier said than done, though. Cory Sills and I were civil to each other now, but we'd never been what you could call friends.

Okay, then my reason for calling her needed to be something at least quasi-official.

Still pondering, I shut off the lights in the coffee shop and closed the door that divided the public part of the store from the kitchen/storeroom space. Tilly was nowhere to be seen, and I guessed that she'd taken off through the cat door as soon as she was done eating her treats.

Which was fine. Since it was a weekday, I hadn't planned on taking her back home with me anyway.

My gaze fell on the two little bistro sets—currently wedged into a corner—that I put outside during the late spring and summer, and it came to me in a flash. For a while, I'd been thinking about trying to get a permit to have a permanent outdoor space on the sidewalk outside the shop, although I'd never gotten around to officially petitioning the city to let me expand my footprint that small amount.

What if I used that possible expansion as my pretext for calling Cory? I could pretend I wanted to pick her brain before I wasted any time on submitting an application to the zoning committee.

I doubted I'd be able to think of a better idea.

Before I could lose my nerve, I pulled out my phone and navigated to the city's website, then touched the link in the directory to connect me to her line. It rang several times before going to voice-mail, which didn't surprise me too much. After all, she was roaming around handing out flyers to ensure her accomplice would be the one elected mayor.

"Hi, Cory," I said. "This is Skye O'Malley. There's something I want to discuss with you. Give me a call back when you have a chance, or you can just stop by the store. Thanks."

I ended the call and headed over to my storage cubby so I could deposit the phone in my purse. As I took off my apron and hung it up, I realized my hands were shaking.

The die had been cast. Now I just had to wait and see where it would fall.

No return phone call from Cory that evening, which I supposed shouldn't surprise me too much. She'd probably gotten back to her office late and decided my call wasn't so important that she couldn't wait until the next morning to return it.

And when I called Deanne to see how she was doing, Mike was the one who actually picked up her phone. He told me she was fine but still pretty zonked—apparently, he had to go pick her up at the dentist because she was in no shape to drive home—and that he'd let her know I'd reached out to check on her.

"But I'm sure she'll be fine to come in tomorrow morning," he assured me.

"Well, if she isn't, tell her to stay home," I replied. "I can manage on my own if I have to."

"I will," he said.

It was sort of aggravating to be carrying around this knowledge and not have anyone to share it with, but I pushed my annoyance out of the way as best I could. Maybe I should have relented and called the police, and yet I could only imagine the resulting fallout if all my wild theories proved to be nothing more than that. Right now, the only real evidence I had was the testimony of a talking cat, and I kind of doubted that sort of allegation would be admissible as evidence. The last thing I needed was to have the town pissed off at me for falsely accusing a dead man's brother of being involved in his murder.

So I forced myself to go about my usual evening rituals of a simple dinner and a glass of wine, followed by some innocuous Netflix viewing before I gave up and went upstairs to bed at a little past eight-thirty. With any luck, Deanne would be fine to come in to work tomorrow, and then I could spill my guts and ask for her advice as to what I should do next.

I checked my phone as soon as I woke up before dawn the next day, but I didn't have any missed calls. Most likely, Deanne was waiting to get out of bed and move around a bit before she decided whether or not she was feeling up to working a full day.

Pushing back my annoyance—after all, my friend didn't have any control over how her body reacted to anesthetics, and so I shouldn't be irritated with her—I got in the shower right away, then went downstairs to make coffee and some breakfast. Back up to brush my teeth and do my usual minimal makeup of mascara and gloss, and then I was out the door at a little past five-thirty.

The sun wouldn't rise for another hour, but I was used to driving to work in the dark. In a way, I enjoyed being up before everyone else, of getting to enjoy the world while it was still hushed and dim, before the busyness of everyday life intruded.

Tilly was actually asleep in her bed as I entered the storeroom, but got up and stretched just as soon as I put my purse in its cubby. "Tuna?" she asked hopefully.

"Nope," I replied as I got down a can of chicken and rice for her. "That's a treat reserved for when you're staying at my place."

She didn't look too thrilled by that answer, but at least she didn't protest, and only waited off to one side while I opened a can for her and dumped it into her bowl. After refreshing her water, I went and gathered the ingredients for today's muffins—blueberry, pumpkin chocolate chunk, and cranberry—and started mixing up the batter. Once the muffins were in the oven and I'd set out the pans for the croissants, which were next up after the muffins were done, I thought it safe to go out into the shop and start getting things ready for opening, since I didn't know when or if Deanne was going to make it in to work.

My hasty clean-up of the day before meant I had a couple of bags of trash I needed to take out to the dumpster behind the building. Holding back a sigh, I grabbed a bag in each hand and headed outside, where the sky had begun to lighten toward gray, signaling we weren't too far from sunrise.

I'd just tossed both bags of trash and was about

to head back toward the shop's rear door when a man emerged from behind the dumpster and grabbed me by the arm.

"Hello, Skye," Dave Gallegos said. "We need to talk."

CHAPTER 16

Partners in Crime

"We've got nothing to talk about," I said, willing myself to be calm even though my heart had started pounding a mile a minute and adrenaline zinged along every nerve ending. "Let go of me!"

His grip only tightened. "No, I don't think so. Inside."

And then he all but hauled me along the alley and up the back stairs into the storeroom/kitchen at the rear of my shop. Tilly was nowhere to be seen—I figured she'd taken off exploring as soon as she was done with her breakfast—and the air was filled with the sweet aroma of baking muffins.

However, I didn't find anything remotely comforting about my current circumstances.

"All right," Dave said, his tone oddly reasonable, considering he'd just frog-marched me down the alley and into the building. "Let's talk. How much?"

"How much what?" I returned, not sure what he was driving at.

"How much to keep your mouth shut?" he asked. A pause, and he sent me a considering look. "It was the tea leaves, wasn't it? That's how you figured it out? That's what Cory told me, anyway."

Damn it. And here I'd thought I was being so clever. Obviously, my vague call to Cory hadn't been quite vague enough. Somehow, she'd figured out that I wanted to talk about something very different from getting zoning approval for an outdoor dining area for my shop.

All the same, I thought I might as well try to play dumb.

"I don't know what you're talking about," I said, doing my best to look wide-eyed and completely innocent. "And I need you to let go."

His eyes narrowed. "No, I don't think so. Not until I know you're not going to go blabbing all over town."

I blinked. "Blabbing what?"

"You want to make this hard on yourself, fine." His fingers clutched my arm even harder, so hard I knew I was probably going to have a ring of bruises on my bicep. All of the friendly, folksy demeanor he'd worn at the town meeting last week had disappeared as if it had never existed at all.

Which it hadn't. Not really. It had all been an act, and I knew I was looking into the eyes of a killer.

"I won't say anything," I said quickly. An utter lie, of course, but I was only trying to get him to let me go long enough so I could grab my phone, or maybe make a run for the security system panel on the wall next to the back door. If I could just reach the panic button....

Dave gave me a thin-lipped smile. "Yeah, right. You really expect me to believe that?"

"It's the truth," I replied, knowing I sounded desperate. But maybe that was a good thing. Maybe my worry and my fear would make my statement a little more believable.

A flicker of what might have been regret came and went in his dark eyes. "It would have been better if you were willing to make a deal. I know money would have made you keep quiet, since then you'd also be an accomplice. As it is—"

He let go of my arm—but only so he could try to wrap both hands around my throat. Entire body thrumming with panic, I somehow managed to take a step or two backward, eluding his reaching fingers even as I saw possible salvation out of the corner of my eye.

My fingers grabbed the edge of one of my heavy cast-iron baking pans, and I lifted it from the

table where I'd been about to prep the croissants
and lobbed it right at Dave's head.

It connected—but only against his ear and the
top of one cheekbone. Still, he staggered from the
blow...before making a leap toward me, face red
with fury.

That hadn't gone well.

His hand caught hold of my sleeve and he
yanked, sending me tumbling to the floor. Landing
on the wooden surface with so much force sent a
shockwave through my body, but I knew I had to
ignore the pain, had to keep scrabbling in an effort
to stay out of arm's reach.

No such luck. He caught hold of my ankle, and
I kicked as hard as I could. Unfortunately, he didn't
let go, but only reached out with his other hand so
he could restrain both my legs.

At that exact moment, the back door opened. I
caught a brief glimpse of my friend Deanne silhou-
etted against the pale dawn light, and had just the
faintest impression of her mouth opening in a
shocked "O" before she reached out with her free
hand and slammed it against the panic button on
the alarm panel. It immediately started to sound—
and also sent a silent signal to the police station
that something was very wrong at Levitation
Latte.

However, she obviously wasn't content to wait
for the cavalry to arrive. Instead, she bolted toward

Dave, her purse dangling from one hand, looking like a Valkyrie about to rush into battle.

Now, my bestie was the kind of person who carried everything except the kitchen sink in her bag. Hairbrush, makeup, travel toothpaste and brush, cell phone, notebook, pens, tissues, mini first aid kit—if it was something a person might remotely consider stashing in their purse, Deanne had it in there. I used to tease her that she was going to make herself permanently lopsided if she didn't remember to switch the shoulder her purse hung on from time to time.

All fifteen pounds plus of that purse went swinging right at Dave's head, impacting with a *crack* that probably could have been heard from across the street. He went down for the count, landing with another, smaller *crack* as his skull hit the floor.

For a second, utter silence reigned in the kitchen. Then I awkwardly pushed myself up to a standing position, taking inventory as I moved of all the bruises that were probably going to form later in the day.

Deanne's startled eyes met mine. "Skye, what the heck is going on?"

I looked down at Dave's prone form. To my relief, his chest was rising and falling, but it definitely looked as though he wouldn't be going anywhere anytime soon.

"He's the one who killed Tom Gallegos," I told Deanne, and her eyes widened even further.

"His own brother? But...why?"

"Some kind of real estate deal, I think," I replied, then shook my head. "I don't know all the details, but it sounded like Dave was pressuring Tom to sell Jaramillo Field so they could make some serious pocket change. Then Dave killed his brother when he wouldn't budge, figuring that he could do whatever he wanted when he was elected mayor."

"'Mayor,'" she repeated, even as sirens began to shrill outside on the street, getting closer.

Well, better late than never.

Then Deanne put a hand to her mouth. "Oh, my God—the election is today!"

"I know," I said, and gave her a grim smile. "Good thing we caught him early in the day, right?"

For a second, she just stared at me. Then, even as someone pounded on the front door of the shop, calling out, "Police! Open up!", she matched my smile with one of hers.

"Definitely a good thing."

Kyle was one of the deputies who'd responded to the alarm, and who looked suitably shocked when I panted out a quick explanation of what had happened. Dave was still unconscious, so Kyle and two other deputies cuffed him and then carried him out between them, his feet dragging along the floor as they went.

I was worried that a lot of people had already cast their ballots, and it seemed quite a few of the town's residents had done that very thing...but not so many that the town would have to deal with the embarrassment of voting in a murderer for mayor. After all the votes were tallied, Alex Donnelly, the deputy mayor, squeaked past Dave Gallegos with only seventy-eight votes to spare.

It was enough, though. And once I was done telling Kyle my story, he quickly radioed the station, letting them know they needed to send a car over to arrest Cory Sills.

They caught her just as she was about to head out the door for work, and, according to what I heard later, had seemed almost resigned as they put handcuffs on her and whisked her away to the police station.

She must have made some kind of deal with the D.A., because she pleaded guilty to a lesser second-degree felony as an accomplice after the fact and was sentenced to five years in prison...meaning she would probably be out in only a couple of years. However, I kind of doubted she'd be able to return to Las Vegas and carry on as though nothing had happened.

People around here had long memories.

Dave Gallegos, on the other hand, was arraigned on suspicion of first-degree murder and was currently awaiting trial. Since Cory had already testified against him, he definitely wasn't going to get off easy, but he'd still decided to let a jury decide his fate rather than cop a plea and face the music right away.

In fact, Cory requested a meeting with me after her sentencing, right before she was due to be sent off to prison. I'd been a little startled by the ask... but I also thought I knew exactly why she wanted to talk to me.

"It was the tea leaves, wasn't it?" she inquired as soon as I approached her cell. She appeared to be the only occupant of the woman's side of the jail right then, which was probably why the deputy had walked me back there for our chitchat rather than conducting the meeting in one of the interrogation rooms.

I only hesitated for a second. "Yes," I replied. It was only a teensy little lie, after all—the tea leaves had given me my first clues, even if I'd been too dense to understand their significance, that the leaves had shown me a spade because they were trying to tell me the crime had something to do with developing a certain plot of land.

And I also knew there was no way in hell I could ever tell Cory Sills that the piece of evidence which had truly cracked the case wide open had come from a talking cat.

She nodded, as if my answer confirmed something she'd already suspected. "I thought that had to be it," she said. "Especially after you left me that voicemail. I could tell from your tone something had changed, that you must have figured it out somehow."

Not for the first time, I reflected that I really needed to up my game if I was going to continue with this crime-fighting stuff. Being an open book to the criminal element was definitely going to cramp my style.

Rather than respond directly to her comment, I said, "I still don't understand why you did it."

She gave me a very thin smile. Obviously, she wasn't allowed any cosmetics in jail, but she was the sort of person whose bone structure didn't really need them.

"Our cut would have been at least three million, maybe more," she told me. "That made it worth the risk. I wanted to have a real life with Dave, not always struggling to get by on an assistant's salary. And really, none of this would have happened if Tom hadn't been so damn stubborn. He could have been part of the deal and done very well for himself."

"Except he had integrity," I said softly, and Cory shrugged.

"Integrity doesn't pay the bills."

There wasn't really anything left to say after that, and I excused myself and hurried out of the jail so I could get outside and pull in a few breaths of clean, fresh air. I wanted to erase the cold-blooded details of the crime from my brain, how Kyle had told me Dave had strangled his brother with a rope in a shadowy alley a block away from the bandstand, and then hid his body inside a large canvas sack, the sort of thing a gardener might use to store grass clippings, before dumping him over the side of the corn maze. A couple of people actually had seen him in the process of performing this grisly task but had only thought he was bringing more hay to the corn maze...which of course had been his plan all along.

As I stood there on the corner and looked across the street to the park where those horrible goings-on had taken place, the sun shone down brightly from above. The breeze was chilly, though, with a definite bite, telling me Halloween was only a couple of days away.

A Halloween that Tom Gallegos wouldn't get to celebrate with his kids...and all because of greed.

I shook my head, and then walked across the park to my side of the street, where Levitation Latte waited.

Cory Sills was dead wrong. Integrity totally paid the bills...as long as you didn't ask for more than you deserved.

How Max had managed to get the contact information for what looked like everyone in both his and my graduating classes, I didn't know, but he'd packed his spacious ranch house with so many people that they spilled out onto both patios. Not that the size of the crowd was a problem, because he'd made sure to have gas heaters set up in all the outdoor areas, ensuring that everyone should be comfortable no matter how skimpy their costumes might be.

As for what I was wearing....

A week before the party—and the day before my meeting with Cory Sills at the jail—a large box had shown up at the coffee shop, delivered by a FedEx driver. I'd opened it in front of Deanne to reveal folds of white cloth, a metal belt, and white boots.

After I lifted the gown out of the box, I realized exactly what it was—Princess Leia's dress from the original *Star Wars* movie, a costume I'd secretly coveted since I was a kid and watched the film on TV the first time.

A little piece of paper had fluttered out of the folds of the costume.

On it was written a single line.

You know, sometimes I amaze myself.

"Oh, he's definitely got it bad for you," Deanne said, and I could only roll my eyes.

"No, I think it's more that he just wants to have someone whose costume matches his," I told her, even as I knew I needed to keep to myself any details about his recent trips to L.A. to discuss a possible role in the Star Wars franchise.

My suspicions had turned out to be correct, because when I showed up at the party, it was to find Max in a Han Solo costume, complete with gun belt slung low on his hips and a credible imitation of the character's sardonic smile playing around his lips.

"You look great," he'd told me, and I'd just smiled. The costume fit perfectly—I wasn't sure how he'd managed that—and I'd even gotten my long hair wrestled into some fairly decent Princess Leia buns after fussing with them for most of the afternoon.

"Thanks to you," I'd replied.

That had been pretty much the extent of our interactions so far at the party, mainly because his attention had immediately been claimed by some of the other guests. I couldn't really resent that, not when there were probably at least a hundred and fifty people—if not more—wandering around the place.

No, I'd hung out with Deanne and Mike, both of them resplendent in their *Game of Thrones* costumes—although I couldn't really place the character Mike was trying to portray and decided not to ask, lest I display my ignorance—but after a while, the house began to feel stuffy despite the French doors to the patios being open, and I escaped outside to catch my breath and get away from the thumping Halloween-inspired music pounding away in the background.

I didn't think Max had been paying any particular attention to what I was doing, and so I was surprised to see him approach me where I stood at the railing that protected the edge of one patio from the steep hillside below. The night wind caught at the hem of my long dress, fluttering the thin material, and I knew I probably couldn't stay out here for too long.

But I also knew I wasn't going to leave now, not with Max coming over to the spot where I stood and looked out into the darkness, with the house at my back, hiding the lights of my hometown.

"Hey," he said. "Hiding from everyone?"

That might have been exactly what I was doing, but I sure wasn't going to admit it to him. People were surface friendly to me, I supposed, but that was about as far as it went in a lot of those cases.

"No," I replied, hoping I didn't sound too defensive. "Just wanted to get some fresh air." I turned so I faced him where he stood a few feet away from me, the illumination from the bistro lights strung across the patio creating a halo of his light brown hair. A tilt of my head toward the Han Solo costume he was wearing, and I asked, "Is that a clue about the role they want you to play?"

His mouth curved in a lopsided smile. "You know I can't tell you that."

Maybe not, but his hint sure seemed clear enough to me. Rather than point out that glaringly obvious fact, I just shrugged. "Well, if they don't cast you in that role, they're stupid. You'd be great."

He tilted his head slightly, as if acknowledging the compliment, and then came over so he could stand next to me. Not too close—definitely not close enough to initiate any intimacies—but all the same, a little shiver went over me that didn't have much to do with the chill wind blowing across the hilltop.

"I wish I could have been there," he said.

Since we'd already hashed over this topic several times, I only gave a small lift of my shoulders. "It's okay," I said with a grin. "Deanne and her kamikaze purse made short work of the villain."

Max's mouth quirked a little in response, probably at the mental image of my petite blonde friend clocking Dave Gallegos with her handbag of death. "Yeah, I would've liked to see that." Then his smile slipped away, and he added, "You definitely didn't need me to figure out the mystery."

"No," I said, then went on before he could respond, "but I only was able to do what I did thanks to Tilly."

"'Tilly,'" Max repeated, some of the amused light returning to his eyes. "She definitely cracked the case. Any luck getting her to stop talking?"

I shook my head. "No...but she told me she's kind of getting used to it. What I think she's really getting used to is all the wet food I've been feeding her. In fact, she's just fine with spending weekends at my house now, but that might be because I had a cat door put in for her."

Yes, Tilly and I had definitely reached an understanding. That didn't mean I wasn't going to keep trying to reverse the spell, but at least she didn't seem nearly so cranky about it.

"Well, that's good." Max paused there, as if trying to collect his thoughts. When he spoke again, he sounded almost tentative...for him. "So... if any other murders crop up, you're still okay with me trying to lend a hand?"

I didn't even hesitate. "Absolutely! You sure helped out that first time around. But," I added with a grin, "I don't think we're going to have any other murders around here for a long time."

"I'll drink to that," Max said, then stopped and looked down at his hands, both of them noticeably empty. "Well, let's go inside and get ourselves those drinks. Deal?"

"Deal," I replied.

He looped his arm in mine and we went inside. A friendly gesture, I supposed, and nothing more, but for now, I'd take it.

I'd definitely take it.

———

Skye's adventures will continue in *Pastries and Prophecies,* releasing in March 2023.

Also by Christine Pope

LATTES AND LEVITATION

(Cozy Mystery/Paranormal Romance)

Caffeine Before Curses

Muffins After Magic

Pastries and Prophecies (March 2023)

———

UNEXPECTED MAGIC

(Urban Fantasy/Paranormal Romance)

Found Objects

Finders, Keepers

Lost and Found

Finding Destiny (January 2023)

———

HEDGEWITCH FOR HIRE

(Cozy Mystery/Paranormal Romance)

Grave Mistake

Social Medium

Household Demons

Perpetual Potion

Jingle Spells

Wandering Monsters

Uninvited Ghosts

Prophet Motive

Ballroom Bits (April 2023)

THE WITCHES OF WHEELER PARK*

(Paranormal Romance)

Storm Born

Thunder Road

Winds of Change

Mind Games

A Wheeler Park Christmas

Blood Ties

Healing Hands

Wishful Thinking

Smoke and Mirrors

MISS PRIMM'S ACADEMY FOR WAYWARD
WITCHES*

(Fantasy/Academy Romance)

Misspelled

Dispelled

Expelled

PROJECT DEMON HUNTERS*

(Paranormal Romance)

Unquiet Souls

Unbound Spirits

Unholy Ground

Unseen Voices

Unmarked Graves

Unbroken Vows

THE DEVIL YOU KNOW*

(Paranormal Romance)

Sympathy for the Devil

Charmed, I'm Sure

A Wing and a Prayer

Wish Upon a Star

Strange Magic

The Arrangement

Defender

Bad Blood

Deep Magic

Darktide

THE DJINN WARS*

(Paranormal Romance)

Chosen

Taken

Fallen

Broken

Forsaken

Forbidden

Awoken

Illuminated

Stolen

Forgotten

Driven

Unspoken

THE WATCHERS TRILOGY*

(Paranormal Romance)

Falling Dark

Dead of Night

Rising Dawn

THE SEDONA FILES*

(Paranormal/Science Fiction Romance)

Bad Vibrations

Desert Hearts

Angel Fire

Star Crossed

Falling Angels

Enemy Mine

TALES OF THE LATTER KINGDOMS*

(Fantasy Romance)

All Fall Down

Dragon Rose

Binding Spell

Ashes of Roses

One Thousand Nights

Threads of Gold

The Wolf of Harrow Hall

Moon Dance

The Song of the Thrush

THE GAIAN CONSORTIUM SERIES*

(Science Fiction Romance)

Beast (free prequel novella)

Blood Will Tell

Breath of Life

The Gaia Gambit

The Mandala Maneuver

The Titan Trap

The Zhore Deception

The Refugee Ruse

STANDALONE TITLES

Hearts on Fire (Paranormal Romance)

Taking Dictation (Contemporary Romance)

Golden Heart (Gaslight Fantasy Romance)

Night Music: A Modern Reimagining of The Phantom of the Opera (Contemporary Romance)

Ghost Dance: A Sequel to Gaston Leroux's The Phantom of the Opera (Historical Mystery/Romance)

Flight Before Christmas (Fantasy Romance)

* Indicates a completed series

About the Author

USA Today bestselling author Christine Pope has been writing stories ever since she commandeered her family's Smith-Corona typewriter back in grade school. Her work includes paranormal romance, fantasy romance, and science fiction/space opera romance. She makes her home in beautiful Santa Fe, New Mexico.

Christine Pope on the Web:
www.christinepope.com

facebook.com/ChristinePopeAuthor

twitter.com/ChristineJPope

pinterest.com/ChristineJPope

www.ingramcontent.com/pod-product-compliance
Lightning Source LLC
Chambersburg PA
CBHW020407260626
47156CB00007B/2275